'Come here and kiss me.'

It was almost an order.

In another time and place Jacinta might have wanted to continue the argument, explore the beginnings of wonder that they loved each other. Maybe banter with him and pit her wits against his. But the time wasn't right. Every moment was precious now, and she stepped into Jonah's embrace with a sigh of relief. His hand brushed the hair from her forehead as he looked deep into her eyes and she absorbed the sight of his dear face like dry earth absorbing rain.

'In another time and another place I won't always come so placidly, you know,' she whispered as he came closer.

'I'll look forward to it,' he said, and his mouth brushed hers.

DANGEROUS ASSIGNMENT

BY
FIONA McARTHUR

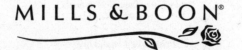

First published in Great Britain 2005
Harlequin Mills & Boon Limited,
Eton House, 18-24 Paradise Road, Richmond, Surrey TW9 1SR

© Fiona McArthur 2005

ISBN 0 263 84301 7

Set in Times Roman 10½ on 12½ pt.
03-0405-43162

Printed and bound in Spain
by Litografia Rosés, S.A., Barcelona

CHAPTER ONE

JONAH ARMSTRONG groaned as he surfaced through the fracturing thinness of his delirium towards the sound.

'Jonah. Can you hear me?'

There was something about the cadence in her voice that calmed him. The nightmare receded as he eased out of the strangling mists and opened his eyes a sliver as he tried to focus.

The face of the speaker was surrounded by a halo of light, which seemed reasonable for an angel, and she must be an angel because he didn't recognise her. Jonah's tongue seemed glued to the roof of his mouth as he tried to speak, and she brought her face closer to hear.

'Melinda's ring,' he whispered, but even his eyelids hurt when he opened them and the struggle with their weight was too great.

Jacinta McCloud, Director of Emergency at Pickford General Hospital, glanced at the man's large, capable hands and tapped the finely wrought signet ring on his little finger. There was a tiny butterfly fashioned from gold on the signet and she shivered at the sight and rubbed her shoe over her ankle where her own tiny tattooed butterfly hid unnoticed. 'There is a ring on your finger, Jonah.'

Her voice again. He sent the message to his brain to open his lids, but the synapses weren't listening. The peppermint of her breath touched his face. 'Jonah, the airline ticket in your wallet says you flew in from Papua New Guinea two days ago and your passport says you spend a lot of time there. When did you take your last antimalarial?'

This time his muscles obeyed and her eyes were dark and caring. He finally articulated his answer. 'Last night. In pocket.'

Jacinta slid her hand into his trouser pocket, retrieved the tablets and read the label. Then she stepped back from the bed and spoke to the nurse beside her. 'If it's malaria, presumably this strain is resistant to Doxycycline. We'll just have to try something else,' she murmured.

When Jonah regained consciousness, he accepted he was finally on the mend. Eyes forced open, he stared at the tiny square of morning light coming from behind the edge of the curtain as if it were a signpost to the normal world. Tentatively he stretched his legs, and although the ache was there, the flooding pain of movement from yesterday had subsided.

Warily he turned his head on the damp pillow as someone approached his bed. Still fuzzy, he squinted to bring the woman's two heads together. Once she'd fused, he could see she had the darkest brows he'd ever seen above brown eyes filled with the compassion he'd noticed yesterday. So she wasn't an angel.

'Good morning, Dr Armstrong. I see your fever's broken.'

Jonah swallowed and licked his lips as he tried to form the words his brain had no trouble coming up with. She must have noticed because she moved swiftly to the bedside table, procured a plastic tumbler of water and directed the straw into his mouth before he even realised he was desperately thirsty.

He sighed as the coolness slid down his throat and the roof of his mouth no longer felt like the floor of a bat cave.

'Thank you.' His voice cracked with weakness and he despised the sound. Still, it was better than being dead.

'The strain of malaria you had was a particularly vicious one and I thought for a while we were going to lose you.'

He could tell she was genuinely glad he was awake, and the knowledge warmed the last of the cold spots in his body. 'Tell me about it.' The idea was vaguely amusing that he could survive tropical snakes, spiders and guerrilla activity in the depths of Papua New Guinea and succumb to a mosquito in the height of civilisation.

'And you are…?' He could feel the strength seeping back into his limbs and there was sweetness to the feeling that reminded him he shouldn't take his body for granted.

'Jacinta McCloud. I'm one of the doctors from the emergency department here at Pickford.'

She smiled and suddenly he was light-headed

again, but this time for a different reason and the old barriers refused to assemble as he'd trained them. Blame the malaria, or fate, or timing because there was something about this woman that slid like a stiletto straight to the core of him in a way he hadn't experienced before.

His life did not include women you couldn't leave behind!

Almost as if she sensed his panic, she turned away and walked to the window. He watched the way she moved, her back ramrod straight like one of those old-fashioned missionary nuns he'd grown up around. Yet somehow it didn't come off. She would always be unmistakably a woman.

And there he was again, speculating about someone outside the parameters of his life. Angry with himself, he pulled his disgustingly weak body upright past the pillow until the cold Formica of the back of the bed was hard against his spine, and he had control.

Jacinta McCloud felt as febrile as this patient had looked the first time she'd seen him, and impulsively she swept back the curtains to allow the morning glow to flood the room. When she slid the window open, cool air damped the heat in her cheeks and memories of yesterday and her first sight of Jonah ran through her mind.

Pushed through the casualty doors by the ambulance personnel, he'd been agitated by the movement of the trolley and she'd spotted him immediately. He'd mumbled semi-audible phrases and the depth of his despair had made Jacinta slip her fingers into his hand to comfort him on his trip to the assessment room.

Strangely, he'd seemed to rest more easily on the bed at her touch, and when the stretcher had stopped and she'd retrieved her hand, he'd twisted his head on the pillow as if searching for the comfort he'd known briefly.

The imprint of his long fingers on hers had burned with more than the man's fever. Not the sort of fanciful notions she was known for.

Then, last night at home when she'd turned out the light to go to sleep, his tortured blue eyes had still haunted her. Almost as if she'd imagined they had some deep connection she'd never known about, which was bizarre, as she was the least fanciful person she knew. Whims and past lives had no place in Jacinta McCloud's busy schedule and neither did malarial-stricken mystery doctors who blew into Casualty. It was probably just the lure of tropical medicine that piqued her interest, not the man.

The breeze from the window tickled her face and brought her back to the present. She'd needed to open the window to create space between them, but now the strength of the sun made her wince. And goodness knew what it would do to Jonah if his eyes were still sensitive to light.

Funny how she thought of him as Jonah and not the Dr Armstrong on his passport. Her fingers balled to pull the curtains again, confused by the thoughtlessness of her actions.

'Leave it open.' His voice was stronger and a tinge

of harshness made her turn and face him. He was sitting upright with his broad chest facing towards her like a teak tree-trunk dissected by a curling trail of fine dark hairs that disappeared down under the sheet. If she was noticing things like that, it was time for her to leave.

She moistened her lips. 'Well, I'm glad you're feeling better. You probably won't see me again as I only dropped in on my way to work to find out how you got on.'

How inane. Jacinta winced and her voice trailed off. This was unlike her. She smiled in the general direction of the bed and averted her eyes as she walked towards the door.

'Call me Jonah.' His voice followed her, the rough edges softened, and she was drawn for one last look. 'Thank you for looking after me, Jacinta.'

He was smiling and she hadn't seen that before, and wished she hadn't seen it now. He changed completely when his white teeth flashed that way above his square chin, and crinkled eyes and self-mocking good humour included her in his warmth. She couldn't help smiling back.

'You're welcome.' She focused again on the door because she had to get out of there before she sank into a chair and just stared at him, dribbling.

'And is there a Mr McCloud?'

She glanced back. There was a beam of sunlight shining off the butterfly on his little finger, and with his tousled hair he looked a little like a pirate. The wicked humour in his eyes amused Jacinta and she looked away to stop herself from laughing out loud. She felt like she'd just downed a glass of champagne—or two.

'I see you're feeling *much* better,' she murmured.

He persisted. 'And the answer would be?'

She looked back at this man who should be still barely conscious, flirting with her as if it were his last two minutes on earth.

'Yes, there is.' She paused. 'My father. Though technically he's a doctor and not a mister. Now I must go.'

'At least drop by this afternoon, Jacinta, and tell me how you guessed so swiftly I had malaria.'

To create a reason to return was tempting and she should be confident she was level-headed enough to be tempted without danger. 'I may be running late. We'll see. Goodbye, Dr Armstrong.'

'Dr McCloud.' He returned her formality and nodded with that supreme confidence good-looking men had.

Jonah watched the door shut behind her and although he listened he couldn't hear her footsteps. But why would he want to hear them?

The smile on his face seeped away and his shoulders slumped into a more relaxed position as he closed his eyes. 'Don't go there, Jonah.' He shook his head at the impossibility of the thought.

Instead of the oblivion of sleep, which he craved, Jonah saw the caring warmth in the dark brown eyes of Jacinta McCloud, and he knew that somewhere in his chest a need he'd never allowed to surface had shifted. The ramifications of that thought terrified him, but not for himself—for Jacinta.

After the loss of his mother and sister, Jonah had accepted that his road would be a solitary one, but in the brief moments he'd seen her, already this woman had threatened his resolve in a way he would never have believed could happen.

He opened his eyes again and stared at the door. Perhaps she wouldn't come this afternoon and he'd never see her again. That thought made him shift in the bed and he wondered cynically to what lengths he would go to seek her out.

Moving quietly down the corridor in her sensible shoes, Jacinta couldn't help glancing up at the clock and noted the fact that for the first time ever she was late for work. She compressed her lips.

Considering that one of the reasons she'd been appointed very young as Director of Emergency was her reliability, this was all the more reason to stay away from Jonah Armstrong this afternoon.

Fate conspired against her and for the second time in two days a patient with severe headache, fever and chills presented, but this disease baffled them. Malaria tests came back negative, as did those for dengue fever and meningitis. The only clue Jacinta isolated was what appeared to be a black crusted bite, a bite the man's wife said had started as a red mark about a centimetre wide nearly a week ago.

She followed the case when the elderly man, Mr Ross, became critical and was transferred to Intensive Care. Insidiously her brain suggested that perhaps

Jonah Armstrong might have an idea what the problem was.

It was a good enough reason to stand outside his door at four-thirty in the afternoon when she only had thirty minutes to go before the end of her day. Still, she hesitated.

The door opened before she could knock and Jacinta took a step back in shock. Jonah Armstrong stood in front of her, albeit swaying slightly, but still he towered over her and the wall of his chest was imposing at close quarters. She stepped back even further. Lying in bed, he hadn't seemed so big!

When she realised she'd retreated, Jacinta lifted her chin and raised her eyebrows. 'Are you supposed to be out of bed?'

He blinked and she thought again how beautiful his blue eyes were and that was when she knew, without a doubt, she shouldn't have come.

'Good afternoon, Jacinta.' Her name rolled off his tongue as if he'd been practising it, which was ridiculous, then he, too, stepped back and gestured grandly for her to enter, like some old-fashioned butler. 'I'm so pleased you could visit as I may go berserk with my own company in here.'

Compelled against reason, Jacinta walked past him into temptation, but her brain was still functioning in some capacities. 'I could arrange for you to be moved to a four-bed ward, if that would give you the social stimulation you require,' she said.

'I was thinking more like discharge into the real

world but let's put all that to the side and just enjoy each other's company.'

Jacinta was back in control. 'I haven't come for the company, I've come to pick your brains.'

'Even better,' he said, as he gestured for her to sit while he climbed back up onto his bed. He couldn't hide his weariness as he lay back, and Jacinta frowned. It was obvious he wouldn't appreciate her repeating that he shouldn't have been out of bed so she went on.

'I understand you have worked overseas a lot and have a background in tropical diseases.'

He nodded and she went on. 'We have a patient with severe headache, body temperature over forty degrees Celsius, a rash, chills and generalised adenopathy. The only other characteristics seem to be a lesion on his right arm that is now crusted with a black scab and some marked axillary lymph enlargement.'

She looked up to see if he had any suggestions, but he gestured for her to go on.

'Now his pulse rate is going up, blood pressure's coming down and we're getting some muscle twitching and delirium. His condition is now critical.'

He had his hands behind his head and she could tell he was running through the possibilities in his mind. 'Has your patient been to the forest? Did he have a cough?'

'I think his wife mentioned a cough earlier in the illness and they've been back from the Northern Queensland for a week.'

Jonah nodded. 'He's probably been brewing it for a week or more. I'd check him for scrub typhus or tropical typhus. The scab's the give-away. It's from a mite bite and subsequent larvae. You will have to watch for myocarditis, but the illness responds well to Chloramphenicol or Tetracycline.'

Just like that. His knowledge was impressive. Though she didn't delude herself that was all the attraction he held for her. So now what excuse did she have to stay? 'Thank you, I'll pass your thoughts on to the intensive care physician.'

Jacinta stood because she really should go, but one question wouldn't hold her up long. 'How did you become involved in tropical diseases and medicine in the developing world?'

He smiled slowly and sat up to swing his feet over the edge of the bed again so that she wasn't standing over him. His gaze travelled lightly over her face and neck as if to assess her real interest. Jacinta shuddered at what response she would have if he showed her the full force of his charm. Already she was having trouble dragging her eyes away from his face.

'I grew up as one of the MKs. Missionary kids.'

His voice had dropped to a deep rumble and Jacinta accepted that his rich tones fascinated her. She could have listened to him all day.

'MKs have unusual childhoods,' he said with a smile. 'And think it's normal to be one of the only English-speaking people for miles around.

'There're drawbacks, though. Some of the food I've eaten would never appear on a Sydney menu and the general level of hygiene leaves a lot to be desired. As a doctor you see diseases in such an advanced state you can't believe the human body could still move, let alone have just walked a hundred miles to see a doctor.'

He shrugged but his eyes burned with commitment and she could see the real man now.

'My passion is not just for tropical diseases but the progress of diseases in the tropics. I keep going back because otherwise someone else would be even more stretched for time with one less pair of hands. And I do believe I can help.'

Jacinta nodded, aware he'd skimmed the surface of his reasons, and aware also how much she'd love to listen to him talk more of his experiences. Warning to self. Leave now.

'I understand that Papua New Guinea is politically unsettled at the moment. What about the danger?'

He shrugged. 'I wouldn't say that it's too dangerous to work there.' He smiled without humour. 'But it's no place for a non-native woman. I've never thought to get married. Too old to change my ways and it is too risky to have a family. My father found that out after my mother was killed. My sister and I were sent to Sydney to school but I'd already decided to return when I was older. Like my parents, I believe in the heart of the people of the region.'

She wondered about the ring on his finger. He lifted his head as if to shake off the dark memories and looked at her. 'How about you? How did you fall into this profession?'

It wasn't a question she encouraged but she felt obliged to touch on her reasons because he'd answered her curiosity. 'I saw something when I was younger that made me want to be able to prevent unnecessary death where I could. It was easier that my father is wealthy and a doctor as well.'

She omitted the fact that the woman had been her own mother dying in childbirth or that as an orphaned teenager she'd lived in poverty for the next year before her father had found her. The other loss she dared not disturb. Jonah didn't need to know those things.

But she'd spent enough time with him. 'I have to go. Thank you for your suggestion about typhus. I'll pass it on before I leave.'

'Will I see you tomorrow?'

He was watching her and she didn't know where to look. She glanced at her watch and she couldn't believe how much time had passed. 'I don't think so. Look after yourself.' She smiled in his direction and then concentrated on the door.

When she left the hospital ten minutes later she'd contacted the new patient's doctor with Jonah's provisional diagnosis, and further tests were ordered. She hoped definitive treatment would soon be started and the extra confusion she now carried about Jonah Armstrong had been worth the trouble.

Her cat was used to Jacinta being late. That thought made Jacinta smile as she weaved in and out of the peak-hour traffic in her red convertible. The car, a gift from her father as a graduation present, was hot inside and today she felt the need to retract the hood and feel the wind in her hair.

She'd tossed her white coat hurriedly onto the tiny back seat and kicked her shoes off to drive in her stockinged feet and she wondered why she'd never done that before.

There was something sensually liberating about driving home like this, with her hair lifting in the breeze and her toes in direct contact with a responsive gas pedal.

She bumped over the ridge where her driveway met the road and pulled up to wait for the automatic garage doors to open. She could see her cat prowling the front windows behind the curtains.

As she let herself into the house, the phone was ringing. Moggy, her half-grown Siamese, wound its legs around hers in disapproval at the lack of companionship. She had half an hour to eat before she had to go out to the youth refuge. Jacinta sighed.

She picked up the phone on the way to the fridge. It was her stepmother, Noni, and Jacinta tucked the phone under her neck to listen as she lifted the sealing plastic wrap from a prepackaged meal and paused to glance at the calendar before she slid the dish into the oven. It must be nearly time for her stepmother to descend for her monthly stopover.

'Yes, I had a good day. How're Dad and the kids?'

Noni's throaty chuckle echoed down the line. 'Fine, but we haven't seen you for ages. I'd like to come down next weekend to visit if that's OK.'

Jacinta smiled. 'When is it not OK? I thought you

must be due for a stay.' Jacinta could feel the familiar guilt creep over her.

Noni would have preferred Jacinta to drive the five hundred kilometres to Burra for a change, but that trip always made Jacinta's heart ache to return to the place where her happiest memories were.

Burra was where she'd met Noni, the midwife her father had taken her to when he'd first found out that he had a teenage daughter and that she was pregnant.

It must have been premonition that had made Jacinta's mother try to contact Iain McCloud to tell him about seventeen-year-old Jacinta. Adele had died of a congenital heart defect when giving birth to a late child before the letter had found Iain, and Jacinta had been left homeless for almost a year.

Used to making do, and unaware she had a father, Jacinta had moved into a communal house where she'd found the true meaning of destitution. When she'd fallen pregnant, her boyfriend had left her and she cared little for her own health or that of her un-born child, naïvely believing she would die, like her mother, when she gave birth.

One day, in the dismal squats she lived in, a well-dressed man appeared, claimed he was her father and whisked her off to his harbour-front home. Initially, the relationship between father and daughter hadn't worked, and Iain McCloud had removed his daughter from Sydney to get away from her past.

For Jacinta, the change from the daily struggle for food and hygiene to being under the care of a man who could provide everything she needed, except her mother, was surreal. Why couldn't this man have come to find them seventeen years ago?

It wasn't easy for either of them until they met Noni, Jacinta's antenatal teacher, who later became her father's wife. In the guest house run by Noni's aunt, Jacinta learned to love her father and finally gave birth to her own beautiful daughter, Olivia.

Burra contained all the best memories of Jacinta's life after her mother died. Memories also of those magical few weeks with her infant daughter, Olivia, before they discovered she had the same congenital heart defect that had killed her grandmother.

The best heart surgeon in Sydney agreed to operate but the prognosis was poor. And so it proved.

Olivia succumbed, and after her tiny daughter's death Jacinta never forgave herself for not caring more during her pregnancy despite the assurances of everyone that Olivia's condition had been predetermined. As a final farewell, she had a tiny butterfly tattooed on her ankle in memory of her daughter.

Then she threw herself into study to become a doctor with her father and stepmother's support, and her off-duty hours were spent at a teenage refuge where she formed friendships with many young women going through the same dilemmas she'd faced before she'd met her father.

Though, lately, Noni had been hinting that Jacinta should look for another life apart from commitment to work and welfare, and her stepmother had begun a campaign of gentle harassment.

Take up travelling, get a pet. Jacinta looked across

at the sky-blue eyes of her cat and shook her head ruefully. Noni's words flowed over her as Jacinta-the-doctor turned into Jacinta-the-stepdaughter.

'When are you due for a holiday?' Noni asked.

'I can't take a holiday. You gave me a cat.'

Noni chuckled again. 'We can mind the cat. You need a break.'

Jacinta would have loved to have seen her father's face when Noni said that. He was not a cat person. Her smile faded. She couldn't see herself as a lady of leisure. The last ten years since she'd moved to Sydney had been such a rush with uni, then the long hours of residency, then even longer hours as Emergency Registrar at Pickford, until she'd finally earned her position as Director of Emergency.

To be appointed Director had been her ambition, and she'd followed it single-mindedly, like everything else she'd done since the death of her daughter. She'd assumed she would be in that job for a long time to come, so why now was she so suddenly unsettled? She wouldn't know what to do with free hours more than once a week. She glanced at the clock. Today was turning into a day that was characterised by her being late.

Jonah Armstrong's face flashed into her mind. The day had been characterised by something—or some-one—else as well.

'I met an interesting man today.' She didn't know why she said it, but the silence at the other end of the phone confirmed she had. She winced at the speculation that statement would cause, so hurried on before Noni could form any questions.

'Give my love to everyone. I'll ring you later tonight if I get home at a reasonable hour, but I have to go now.'

Jacinta put the phone down, opened the screen door and let a bell-collared Moggy out for a few minutes before she crossed the hall to climb the stairs. She noticed the plant Noni had given her last month was wilting badly. She really must water it.

Her father had often said she tried to jam too much into her life, but Jacinta had no doubt that life was fickle and she was covering all her bases. He hadn't been there to watch Adele kill herself to feed and clothe their daughter.

Maybe Iain McCloud wouldn't have allowed their hardship if he'd known of his daughter's existence, and he had been there for the last twelve years, but Jacinta wasn't prepared to take from him for ever.

It was almost a penance to her mother that, although she had joined the ranks of the wealthy when her father had found her, she'd decided to rely only on that wealth until she could stand on her own two feet. Her father had a new family to be responsible for and Jacinta loved them. But they were five hundred kilometres away and his family, not hers. Olivia had been her family.

She glanced around at the home she'd made and finally realised she'd met her own expectations. The trouble was today, it seemed, she was rattling around among her own possessions.

She was a twenty-nine-year-old, fully qualified career-woman with a healthy savings account and the freedom to do what she wanted.

Empty days and nights.

Jacinta sank into her chair and stared out the window, the TV dinner forgotten on the bench. She'd achieved what she'd set out to do so why was she so unsettled today? How could she jolt herself out of the doldrums?

CHAPTER TWO

'TROPICAL diseases and travel.' Jonah Armstrong shrugged those massive shoulders and all the nurses sighed as if he'd taken off his shirt like a superstar tennis player at the change of ends.

Jacinta caught the conversation as she arrived for work the next morning and she smiled grimly to herself. There but for the grace of God sigh I, she thought, and pretended not to see him.

'Dr McCloud.' Jonah pretended no such thing. 'Just the lady I was looking for.' As a signal to break up a gathering it worked well, and the nursing staff drifted away with only a few backward glances.

Jacinta consciously locked away the woman inside herself and concentrated as a doctor. She looked him up and down critically. 'I gather you're well enough to be discharged today.'

In her opinion he looked pale, with a faint yellowish tinge to the darkness of his skin. Still, she didn't doubt the strength of his constitution could shake off the lingering effects from the fever if he took it easy enough.

'I won't be hitting the pub and abusing my liver for a while, if that's what the appraisal was for.' He was remarkably close to the mark and Jacinta had to smile.

'Hopefully you'll give it a month before you fly anywhere with malarial mosquitoes,' she said.

'I won't be rushing out of Sydney for the next couple of weeks.' His next words took them both by surprise. 'If I find any interesting tropical diseases, can I give you a call?'

Startled, Jacinta looked straight into his eyes. 'You know where I am, Monday to Friday.'

'I was thinking about the weekend.' The answer was so quick she couldn't think of a refusal or prevent the heat in her cheeks. What did she want to do? It had been so long since a man she fancied flirted with her. She frowned. Now she was admitting she fancied him?

She had male friends but friendship was the last thing she felt around Jonah. The intended brevity of his visit to Sydney made him safer than he could have been.

Jonah's tone was measured. 'I understand that you could be reluctant to give a stranger your phone number.'

Jacinta couldn't help be intrigued by the life he must have led while she'd been rushing from home to work and back again. He was just so different and lately she'd felt so dull.

'It's unlikely you'll catch me but perhaps we'll manage to get together before you go back.' She didn't know why she'd piqued his interest and it was the last thing she needed to do when she was trying to tell herself she wasn't interested in him. Still, it was reassuring to know she could be attractive to a handsome man.

Jacinta glanced away to the emergency entrance but there was no distraction there except for the administrator who smiled when he caught her eye and started towards them. Jonah picked up the hint and held out his hand.

Before the other man could get too close, Jacinta weakened. 'I'm under J. McCloud, Bondi Beach, in the phone book.'

He nodded and took her fingers in his. 'I just came to say goodbye and thank you.' He pulled a card out of his pocket for the medical corps he worked for and transferred it into her palm. 'If you have a tricky fever like yesterday, feel free to give me a call or e-mail me. Try the mobile, and if I'm around I'll be more than happy to discuss the case with you.'

Her fingers curved around the card gingerly. 'Thank you. I'll put you on the Rolodex as a resource,' she said as the other man came up beside her.

Jonah smiled blandly at them both, and after one last lingering look in Jacinta's direction he nodded and turned away. The sound of approaching sirens almost cleared him from her mind and she dived thankfully back into harsh reality. He wouldn't ring.

When Jonah returned to his hotel room and threw his keys on the Italian hallstand, he felt chilled by the impersonal look of the room. He really should make a permanent base in Sydney to call home.

But first he should ring his employer and give himself a couple of weeks' sick leave because the last thing they needed was for him to become delirious a hundred miles from the nearest airstrip and die on them. It was too hard to find replacements.

It wasn't the first time he'd contemplated establishing a home in Sydney, but this was the strongest he'd felt about it for a while. He could always leave a house to the mission when he died. He'd spent the last ten years flitting around the world, staying with friends for his short breaks and in hotels when he felt antisocial.

Most of his off-duty time he'd spent hunting up supplies and endorsements that kept the tiny hospital in Papua New Guinea that he worked in from closing. He didn't actually own a home where he could have his own things around him and put his feet up without having to be polite to anyone.

He grimaced at the unattractive picture of himself he'd just painted. He could sell a few of those shares his father had bought for a rainy day and still live well off the dividends. Then he could lend the house out to colleagues who needed a break.

He had a handful of friends who were property developers but he'd have a look for himself first. Tomorrow, when he had more stamina.

There was something about Sydney he enjoyed, more so after this morning, and he wondered just how much was to do with a certain dark-haired, dark-browed, dark-eyed doctor.

It was funny how clear Jacinta was in his mind and

the thought brought a frown to his face. It was unlike him to be persistent towards someone who didn't know his rules.

He'd long ago decided to avoid serious relationships, and despite the growing tourist industry, he was still under the opinion that PNG was too dangerous to take a family to live. Melinda had reminded him of that. He winced as the familiar guilt twisted his gut and stroked the ring on his finger. They'd been so idealistic and foolish and his sister had paid the price.

He was too old to change his ways and become a regular worker like that fellow at Pickford making eyes at Jacinta.

Unable to sit with his thoughts, Jonah stood to pour himself a drink then remembered his joking promise to Jacinta that he wouldn't abuse his poor liver for a few weeks. He smiled cynically and replaced the tiny bottle of Scotch in the bar fridge before taking himself off to shower away the dark thoughts.

Depression was a normal sign after a serious illness, he mocked himself.

The next morning Jonah began to scan the real estate section of the internet on his laptop. It was funny how his eyes were drawn to those properties for sale in Bondi.

On the Sunday of the following week the phone rang in the McCloud house and Noni, Jacinta's stepmother, down for the weekend, picked it up.

'Jacinta, it's for you. He says his name is Jonah.'

Jacinta glanced in the mirror and saw the confusion in her eyes. How was she to deal with this? She'd spent the last week reassuring herself he wouldn't ring. He was a fly-by-nighter in town for a few weeks. At best she'd be a diversion for him and at worst she could lose her heart. No, she wouldn't. He was interesting and she really did want to find out more about his work.

Risky but attractive. 'OK. I'll be there in a minute.' She pulled the towel from the rail and wrapped it around herself, then turned the tap on again to rinse cold water against suddenly hot cheeks.

She really hadn't thought he'd ring.

Noni's voice drifted up to her. 'I think he was on a mobile because it just cut out.'

Jacinta sagged back against the vanity and closed her eyes. Maybe it was a sign, though she didn't believe in signs. If he rang again she'd say she was going out for the day. This much confusion from one phone call could only spell trouble. He probably wouldn't ring back.

The sound of the doorbell five minutes later had her heart bounding in her chest. She'd always wondered what palpitations had felt like. And she'd bet it was Jonah Armstrong that showed her.

'Do you want me to get that?' Noni called out from the kitchen, and Jacinta didn't know what to do.

'I'll get it,' she said, and dashed into the bedroom to pull on a sundress that didn't require a bra to be modest.

It was her fault that Jonah had turned up at the house. She'd been the fool who'd told him she was in the phone book.

She dragged a comb through her hair and whipped the back of it into a ponytail.

The doorbell rang again and this time there was no comment from Noni. Jacinta trod slowly down the stairs and across the hall, and she paused before opening the door to look through the security peephole. It was Jonah all right.

She opened the door and glared at him. 'I'm not impressed at you just turning up, Dr Armstrong.'

She was scowling at him and he thought she looked gorgeous. Jonah could see he had some ground to make up, but he was thrown by the way her damp fringe curled around her face and her ponytail, which dripped a rivulet of water down her long neck.

He had to physically restrain himself from brushing the droplets away so his first attempt at conversation was less than inspired. 'My phone died and I was outside when I rang.' He shrugged. 'It was an impulse. I'm looking at a house in the next street and thought you might come with me.'

He was babbling but the sundress she had on moulded itself to her figure like a second skin and she was all legs and subtle curves. His chest tightened as he drew in a breath.

'I'm still not impressed.' She repeated herself but the scowl had eased. He tried a smile.

'It's the ladies of the house.' He spread his hands helplessly. 'They regard me suspiciously if I come on

my own. I need a chaperone.' He glanced into the
house behind her. 'You could bring the lady I spoke
to on the phone with you.'

Jacinta narrowed her eyes. 'My stepmother is visiting for the weekend.'

He took a step back and surveyed her. 'I really did
want to ring you first to check if it was OK to call
around, but the phone died before I could get to you.'

'Hmmm.' Jacinta glanced at her wrist but she
hadn't had time to put her watch on. 'We're going
out shortly.'

He looked at his own watch. 'It's nine o'clock and
I'll only take a few minutes of your time.' Jonah
didn't know why it was so important to win this battle
but suddenly he was very reluctant to lose. He
couldn't remember the last time such a pursuit had
mattered.

'Oh, all right,' she said. It wasn't gracious but it
was a win. One point for the male of the species, he
thought, and couldn't help his grin.

He followed her into the house and it was so much
warmer than the hotel. Jacinta's home was open plan,
very feminine and restful with lots of cane and soft
lounges. Magazines were scattered across the coffee-
table and a couple of terminally ill house plants wilted
quietly in the corner. He didn't know why he found
that appealing, but he did.

'I see you have a green thumb.'

She looked at him from under her magnificent
brows and scowled at him again. 'It's my forte.'

Jacinta stopped at the bottom of a curved staircase

and he began to realise that he wasn't in her class financially. He wasn't sure how he felt about that because it was something he'd never thought about before.

She called towards the sound of someone stacking dishes. 'Noni, could you come through for a minute, please?'

When she arrived, the woman was tiny, blonde and had a mobile face that made him want to smile. Not quite the evil stepmother he'd envisaged.

Jacinta introduced him to the petite woman. 'Noni, this is Dr Jonah Armstrong. He's over from Papua New Guinea for a few weeks and wants my company while he looks at some real estate. Apparently the house is in the next street so I won't be long.'

Noni smiled and held out her hand as if she'd known Jonah for years. 'It's lovely to meet you, Jonah.' Jacinta watched Noni glance up and down the full height of him and she even patted his hand. Jacinta was worried that Noni would invite him for lunch the way she was eyeing him, but then she saw the funny side of her stepmother's approval and stifled a laugh.

She stepped between them. 'I'll be back soon.' She hugged her stepmother and turned to Jonah. 'Lead on, Dr Armstrong, and I'll look at this house with you.'

The home they looked at was on an impossibly steep block with an overgrown jungle anywhere there wasn't a rockface, but it had magical views out to sea from a turret window and the front veranda. The previous owner had even had a telescope set up, and the furnishings in the house weren't far from the nautical either. It was a man's home and there wasn't a lady of the house to be seen anywhere.

So much for requiring a chaperone! Jacinta rolled her eyes.

Then she noticed that Jonah seemed to be spending more time looking at her than the property he was supposed to be interested in, but she was enjoying herself hugely. Jonah's sense of humour had her giggling when she least expected it and there was something off-beat about the house that made her wonder if it wasn't perfect for him.

The crusty executor officiously showed them over the property and each corner held a new curiosity. The house was being sold with contents, and for a man with few possessions it was an easy way out for Jonah.

When they returned to the car, Jonah was silent as he drove her home in his hired vehicle. Jacinta glanced across at his profile but she couldn't read his expression. It was strange to be sitting across from a man she barely knew after something as personal as looking at real estate together.

She wondered what he was thinking. 'Well? What were your thoughts on the house?'

'Fine.' Jonah stared straight ahead.

Too noncommittal. She frowned. 'You don't sound sure.'

He took his eyes off the road for a second and glanced at her with a rueful smile. 'I've never owned a house. It's quite a commitment.'

Jacinta shrugged. 'So you're a commitmentphobe. If you decide you don't want to live there you could rent it out. Property likc that will appreciate in value.'

He risked another glance. 'You sound very savvy about the property market.'

She looked away, not willing to go into details about her paranoid need for security. A legacy from too many bills and not enough money with her mother. 'Isn't everyone nowadays?'

'I like the house.' He suddenly grinned. 'I love the house and all the crazy bits that go with it. I just find it so sad that someone has put their whole life into creating their home and it can be bought by a passer-by as a packaged item.'

Now she understood. 'I don't see it like that. The owner of that house had a full and interesting life, obviously different to that of your average man, and probably with philosophies a lot in common with yours. I think he'd be pleased to see someone like-minded adding their life experiences to his.'

The car slowed and Jonah looked at her. 'Where on earth do women come up with things like that?' He looked back at the street and shook his head. 'Don't get me wrong. I love the concept—but the guy is dead.'

Jacinta rolled her eyes. 'He lives on in his house.'

'Oh, great, there'll be two of us living there.' Jonah snorted.

Jacinta couldn't help the giggle that started way down in her stomach. She loved it. She loved the craziness of the conversation, and being around Jonah made her feel alive.

Jonah looked back at her. 'What do you think? Should I buy the house even though it's haunted?'

'Yes. I liked the turret room and it probably has secret passageways.'

Jonah started to laugh. 'I should have known you'd say that. But that proves it. The three of us think I should buy the house—and that includes the guy who haunts it.'

'If it's haunted, at least the house won't be lonely when you're away.'

Jonah nodded his head judiciously. 'So true.'

Jacinta could contain her curiosity no longer. 'So tell me about where you've worked and how long you've been a foreign aid doctor.'

'I've been working for the medical arm of Missions Pacific for about ten years. My parents were missionary doctors before they died and I grew up in out-of-the-way villages in Papua New Guinea before my sister and I came to Australia for boarding school.' He shrugged. 'PNG was a little less politically interesting then, but if you're careful it's still a wonderful country.'

He turned into Jacinta's driveway and she decided it was worth the risk of more time spent with him. 'Would you like to come in for coffee?'

He looked at her and there was a twinkle in his eyes. 'I thought you were both going out.'

'We can go this afternoon.'

Twenty minutes later the three of them sat in the

den and Jacinta and Noni listened in fascination to Jonah's description of remote villages, exotic wildlife and medical emergencies managed with the barest essentials.

Jacinta couldn't get enough. 'So is your sister still in PNG?'

'She's dead.' The words hung in the air as if he needed to impress himself as well as her. 'But, yes, she was buried over there.'

Jacinta paused, horrified at her blunder. 'I'm sorry.' She frowned as something else he'd said at the hospital made more sense. 'Is her death why you say it's too dangerous for families?'

'A lot to do with it, though the Papuans on the whole are a happy people.'

'Tell me about Pudjip. How big is the hospital?'

Jonah's eyes took on a far-away look. 'A hundred beds. It's not big but it's busy. We see four hundred inpatients and four thousand outpatients a month.' He smiled at the memories and then looked back at her, and she was glad to see his darkness had lifted.

'It's not just tropical diseases either. We do everything, and I mean everything. We have eighty to ninety obstetric deliveries and sixty to seventy major surgical procedures, as well as chemotherapy, paediatrics and health screening.'

Jacinta sighed. 'I've always been fascinated by medicine in the developing world. It sounds very different to what I do now.'

Jonah lowered his brows. 'It's no place for a woman.'

'I'm sorry about your sister, but welcome to the twenty-first century, Dr Armstrong. Women can do anything a man can do.'

'Oh, it would be an adventure all right, Dr McCloud,' he mimicked her, 'but I think there are specific dangers for women.' His face was grim.

'It still sounds like paradise.'

'It's primitive, unsanitary in a lot of the villages, stinking hot and the mosquitoes try to kill you all the time.'

'You seem to like it well enough. Are you attempting to scare me off being attracted to PNG?' Jacinta baited him and he bit back.

'Are you interested enough that I have to worry?'

She tipped her chin up. 'It's really none of your business what I do so you don't have to worry.'

They glared at each other.

Noni looked at them as each tried to stare the other down, and she jumped when the phone rang. 'I'll get it,' she said, and the relief in her voice was patently clear.

She glanced at Jacinta as she went to answer it then her voice drifted in from the kitchen. 'It's your father.'

Jonah stood up when Jacinta did. She held out her hand and smiled. 'Thank you for an interesting morning, Jonah.'

He smiled grimly and took her fingers in his. 'Thank you for coming with me to see the house. Goodbye, Jacinta.' He looked towards the kitchen. 'Please, say goodbye to Noni for me.'

Jacinta preceded him to the door and stood beside it to see him out. 'I will.'

Jonah walked down the path and slid into his hire car. It had been a disquieting morning.

There'd been flashes of delightful amusement as they'd bantered, and when he'd met Jacinta's eyes it was as if they'd known each other for years. He couldn't deny he was fiercely attracted to her and he didn't think she was immune to him. Kindling her interest in Papua New Guinea had been a foolish thing to do and he regretted it immensely. Jonah frowned as he reversed out of the driveway.

All he could hope for was that she was dreaming, all talk and no action, but his instincts told him she was the wrong woman for that. He'd seen her eyes narrow and the speculative look she'd given him when he'd said Pudjip was no place for a woman.

Still, she had a good job that she couldn't possibly leave, so she was safe. Which was just as well, because she was a fascinating woman and the thought of her day in and day out at Pudjip was unsettling.

He'd love to know Jacinta's background, and what made Jacinta McCloud tick.

Jonah steered the car towards the estate agent's to discuss a house that he suddenly had to buy. He had no desire to look at any other property. As soon as the paperwork was organised and signed, he'd head back to work. It was too attractive around here for a single man.

CHAPTER THREE

FOR Jacinta, an idea that had started as crazy soon became an obsession and she began to gather information on outreach medicine and Papua New Guinea in every spare minute. During medical school she'd shone in tropical medicine and the lure of hot steamy places had always seemed particularly exotic to her.

Here was something she could sink her teeth into and meet her need for a change. Of course, her decision had very little to do with Jonah Armstrong, but she did think it strange the conversation she'd had with him never left her for long.

While she admitted he piqued her interest, the lure of Jonah was a fleeting thing. She doubted she would ever settle down with a man because they couldn't be trusted to build your life on. She was her own woman and always would be. She had to acknowledge that the possibility of a little more interaction with Jonah was a pleasant thought.

But it was the idea of adventure after twelve years of circumspection that was particularly attractive. Even a little danger wouldn't be out of place in her ordered life.

All she needed to know was how to get involved in the medical side because if she worked overseas only one short term a year she'd been told she could

step down to Deputy Director at Pickford, gain tropical medicine experience they could use and keep her
job.

The day she decided she had enough information
to make an informed decision arrived and there was
no doubt this was what she wanted. Jacinta switched
on her computer and e-mailed the company address
on Jonah's card. If Missions Pacific wouldn't have
her there was always Médecins Sans Frontières.

At the back of her mind she accepted she would
be disappointed if she couldn't work with Jonah's organisation.

Along with the e-mail to Missions Pacific, she
phoned home to Burra.

Her father answered the phone and she smiled at
the warmth in his voice when he realised who it was.
'Hi, Dad.' She plunged straight in. 'I'm thinking of
spending some time in Papua New Guinea.'

She listened to the silence as her father processed
her statement, and he didn't disappoint her with
meaningless protestations.

'That sounds different.'

Jacinta smiled appreciatively into the phone. 'You
always said I should travel.'

'I was thinking somewhere less unstable but I do
hear the scenery is beautiful.' He paused again as if
unsure about his next statement. 'I know how inde-
pendent you are but I do have contacts in the
Australian embassy in Port Moresby. Would you
mind if I phoned them just to set up an emergency
contact if you need it?'

Good old Dad. 'I won't need them as I'm dealing with Missions Pacific, but feel free if it makes you feel better.'

'It would.'

'Fine.' She pictured her father, tall and handsome with a frown on his face as he tried not to tell her what to do. She'd inherited a lot of her father's control needs herself and she understood him.

'So what's the attraction in Papua New Guinea?'

'I met a foreign aid doctor and his passion for the work he does made me realise I hadn't found my niche. I want to make a difference.'

'You do make a difference, Jacinta.' There was pride in her father's voice and she felt the tears sting her eyes. She knew he found it hard that she didn't want to spend more time at Burra.

'Some difference. But in a cushy way.'

'Well, Papua New Guinea should be free of cushiness.' The dryness in his voice was unmistakable. 'But I'm sure you have looked into it. We'll be here if you need us. Hang on.' There was a background conversation and her father laughed. 'Noni said to say hello to Jonah for her and she'll ring you tomorrow.'

Jacinta rang off, shook her head at her stepmother's cheekiness and then sat back and waited to find out if she had a job.

Self-funding meant there was no problem setting her time limit and Jacinta planned on an eight-week period to start with. It would be the adventure of a lifetime.

The next day Missions Pacific returned that they

were willing to accept her and Jacinta asked for placement near Jonah if possible. It seemed crazy not to go for at least the region where she knew someone from the organisation, and it didn't necessarily mean they would work together. Did it?

The next week was a flurry of clothes-hunting, house-sorting and a quick trip halfway to Burra to meet Noni for lunch and the transfer of Moggy into Noni's car.

'Your father will get used to having a cat,' Noni reassured Jacinta, and they both laughed. 'Have you heard from Jonah?'

'I e-mailed him but he hasn't replied. He's possibly on a field trip or the phone lines could be down. Apparently that's pretty common.'

Noni nodded and hugged her. 'Be careful. And as for Jonah, go with what feels right,' she said, and Jacinta kissed her goodbye.

The next day, the Port Moresby humidity hit Jacinta's face like a hot damp towel as soon as she poked her head out of the air-conditioned plane, but February was the end of summer so maybe it would get cooler.

The heat and bombardment of aromas were overwhelming. The scent of bougainvillea, the heavy sweetness of what she later found out to be the betel-nut chewed by the locals, the overlying cloying smell of rotting vegetation and good old-fashioned sweat all vied for her attention.

Strangely it was the brightness of the light and the

vivid reds in the clothes of the native Papuans that
caught her imagination.

Bright green vegetation around the airport made
everything else look ordinary, even the airliner, as she
stepped down onto the steaming tarmac.

When she entered the terminal, huge rotating ceiling fans circulated the crowded bouquet of pungent
aromas and she could feel the excitement in her blood
and the smile on her face.

'Dr McCloud?' Jacinta nodded at a grinning porter
dressed in white. He waved the sign with her name
on it. 'I'm Jimmy Puk Puk from the mission. I'll take
you cross to the MAF plane.' He had the brightest set
of white teeth she'd ever seen, and Jacinta grinned
back.

Dressed in shorts and shirt, Jimmy's feet were dust-
ily bare and he held out his left hand to take her bag.
Her eyes were drawn to the healed stump where his
right hand should have been.

He caught her glance and grinned again. 'That's
why they call me Jimmy Puk Puk. Puk Puk mean
croc, 'cos I took more than his hand when I caught
up with that puk puk.'

Jimmy directed her off to a side aisle and broke
into a melodic pidgin English discussion with the customs officer until they were waved through to another
gateway and back onto the tarmac.

Jacinta had been studying the Papuan pidgin
English at home for the last week, along with a brush-
up on tropical illnesses, and she'd followed a little
of the discussion. It was daunting how much she

couldn't understand. Hopefully when a sick Papuan was trying to tell her where it hurt, she'd be able to get the gist.

Out in the sunlight, Jimmy switched back to English to direct her into a beaten-up open Jeep and helped her climb in.

'Mission car,' he said briefly, and Jacinta wondered if he meant he wouldn't own a bomb like this or he didn't own a car at all. 'We go to other side of airport so you can fly to Mt Hagen.'

Missions Pacific was based east of Mt Hagen at the hillside village hospital at Pudjip, high in the mountains. At least away from the coast malaria was less of a problem, Jacinta thought—though that hadn't helped Jonah, she reminded herself.

When she arrived in Mt Hagen, she'd meet the experienced preceptor who would be ultimately responsible for her settling into the corps, and she hoped he spoke English.

Jimmy drove like a maniac and her fingers whitened on the edge of the door, which she clung to. Macabre images of a long rectangular box containing her corpse being slowly carried off the plane to the accompaniment of drumbeats at Sydney airport made Jacinta shudder and realise how far she was from home and the usual safety of her environment.

How the heck had she arrived at this point? Just why was she here? Jacinta swallowed a half-hysterical laugh as Jimmy almost rolled the vehicle to miss a dog that flew at them from under an old truck, and diverted herself with her reasons.

She'd always been interested in tropical medicine. Jonah had painted a picture that had called to her sense of adventure, though he'd tried hard to convince her otherwise. The thought made her wonder again if attempting this trip was a knee-jerk reaction to Jonah telling her she couldn't do it.

Before she could get too bogged down in self-recriminations they swerved back towards a very much smaller red and white aircraft parked under a tree. It was a shame Jimmy ran over the edge of a basket of chickens as he braked.

Amidst the terrified squawks and flying feathers, vitriolic abuse was hurled at Jimmy, and to a lesser extent Jacinta, from a wizened old woman with a red-stained toothless mouth who sprang out from under the wing of the aircraft to gather her escaping live-stock.

'Kakuruk bugga up,' she screamed.

Jimmy just laughed. 'She say the chook no good now.'

Jacinta climbed shakily out of the Jeep and brushed herself down. One chicken would never lay again and the old lady clucked and hung it from her belt by a thong. Jacinta had a fair idea what would be eaten in the woman's house tonight.

Life was certainly different here.

A dour middle-aged man appeared from the back of the plane and wiped his fingers on his trousers before offering his hand to Jacinta.

'You'll be the doctor for Hagen, then?' His thick

Scottish brogue sounded strange in the steaming environment.

She nodded. 'Jacinta McCloud. Have you been waiting for me?'

'Aye. And I'll be glad to get off the ground before the breeze picks up any more. This way, Doctor.'

He took her suitcase and compact bag and squeezed them in behind the seat then reached down and threw the chicken basket on top of it.

'In you get, Mimi,' he said to the old woman who climbed reluctantly into the back of the aircraft first. 'Mimi had surgery and is flying home with us today.'

Jacinta nodded and smiled at the old lady, who still harboured a grudge about the loss of her chicken and stared inscrutably back.

Great, Jacinta winced. I've made my first enemy. She followed Mimi into the back and waved to Jimmy Puk Puk who smiled cheerfully as he returned to his Jeep.

'Mr McTash very experienced pilot.' Jimmy called out with a big grin. 'You crash, he very experienced. Had many, many crash landing.'

Jacinta stared at Jimmy through the window as the pilot shut her in, and her last sight of Jimmy was of the little man rolling around in his seat, laughing. Too much information, Jacinta thought grimly.

When they were safely in the air she leaned forward towards the pilot to make herself heard. 'Does it take long to get to Mt Hagen?'

'Long way lik lik, as they say,' he said with almost

a smile. 'That means it's not "close to" and it's not "long way more, more yet".'

The guy was a mine of information. Jacinta nodded as if she understood, smiled and then leaned back in her seat and closed her eyes. She should have spent more time on the phrase book.

The flight to Mt Hagen was beautiful, and uneventful except for the panic of Mimi every time the aircraft flew into the slightest turbulence. When Mimi screamed, Jacinta's heart rate would double and the panicked chickens would set up a squawk in caged agitation to create an exhausting in-flight diversion.

Finally Jacinta took Mimi's hand in hers and squeezed it. 'Don't worry, Mimi,' she said. 'We'll be there soon.' Though she wasn't sure if she was reassuring the old woman or herself. Either way, the woman seemed to settle a little with Jacinta's reassurance.

By the time the plane made its approach to what appeared to Jacinta as an extremely short landing strip, she was longing to throw herself on the ground and kiss the moist earth.

It had been a long day.

When she dragged her suitcase across the paddock towards the arrival hall a little later she hoped the next 'Jimmy' would give her a more relaxing ride.

It was still atrociously hot but not as steamy as Port Moresby and she lifted the neck of her shirt away from her skin to let in some of the warm breeze.

Her step faltered as she recognised the familiar figure in the shade of the building and she finally admitted how much she had relied on the chance Jonah would meet her.

He was much taller and sturdier than the native Papuans she'd seen so far, and she was very glad to see him in this unfamiliar environment. She thought he still looked slightly jaundiced but that could have been related to the lack of warmth in his eyes. There was no sign of weakness as he reached over and took her case as if it were filled with cotton balls. He stared down into her face for a moment and she couldn't read his expression. She waited for a smile that didn't come and her stomach sank with disappointment.

'It's a small world, Dr McCloud,' he drawled sardonically, and she realised he was definitely not pleased to see her.

'Too small for both of us, Dr Armstrong?'

'The whims of the well-heeled are strange. Hope you can cope with the lack of amenities,' he said, and Jacinta thought briefly of the squalor she'd lived in after her mother had died.

'I think I'll manage.'

Jonah watched Jacinta lift her chin at his comment and could feel himself softening towards her already. He ran his free hand over his head. This was a bad sign as he'd started the week furious when he'd found out who the new doctor was and had worked his way through that to cold, logical planning on how to make her go home.

He'd considered and discarded several plans that included appealing to her good sense, horrifying her with reality, frightening her with facts on the dangers, or wearing her down with a heavy workload. Then he'd arrived at the more basic idea of just plain carrying her back onto the aircraft she got off. Though, from the little he'd seen of Jacinta, he really didn't think any of the options would work.

He tried to regain some of his decisiveness and glanced down at her as she skipped beside him, trying to keep up. He hadn't wanted her to come but he couldn't wish her gone now. It felt too good just to look at her. She was frowning and those heavy brows of hers were signalling her displeasure as if she'd hoisted a flag. His smile faded when he realised he was thinking already he was glad she had come.

'I'd planned on sending you back as soon as possible,' he growled. 'Unfortunately, my assistant came down with what I suspect is the same kind of malaria I succumbed to, and I've had to ship him out. We'll all have to carry the slack of one man down for a while. You'll stay your term and that includes the Sepik trip I've promised to join.'

He glanced across at her. 'If you're on Doxycycline you'll have to change your antimalarial as they have a resistant strain down there that's knocking them down like flies. Though where you'll be for the next week or two isn't so bad.'

The thought of Jacinta as sick as James filled Jonah's gut with cold dread because he knew how powerless they could be to protect her from disease. He'd just have to be vigilant.

He shook her bag. 'I hope you've got your repellent

and long-sleeved shirts in this bag. If I catch you after sunset in short sleeves I'll personally dress you.'

Cold disappointment settled in Jacinta's stomach. Obviously she'd been mistaken and he'd never liked her. She couldn't even catch a glimpse of the warm and delightful man who'd made her laugh in his grim visage. Jonah towered over her and his implacability made him seem even larger than she remembered.

In fact, he was insufferable. She didn't recall any indication he was a closet dictator in Sydney. Since she'd arrived he hadn't even said hello and his blue eyes were icy with hostility.

Well, she was darned if she was going to let him know he'd disappointed her. 'Quite the little demi-god on your home turf, Dr Armstrong.' Her tone was sweet.

'Responsibility does that to people up here. I hate sending people home in pine boxes.'

The comment was a little too close to her previous thoughts to be banished, and Jacinta began to suspect that perhaps Jonah hadn't exaggerated the risks quite as much as she'd thought.

The good news was he drove considerably better than her last driver, though she felt he sped down the Highland Highway at a more than reasonable speed. It took two hours to travel to their destination and very little was said between them.

By the time they pulled up at the Pudjip Station gates a little before sunset, Jacinta had decided two could play at being distant. He glanced at the sun and she decided the next chance she had she'd slip her

long-sleeved shirt on rather than give him something
to complain about.

Wordlessly she followed him around the side of the
hospital to the huts beyond. Her hut had many louvred
windows, all with fly screens, and very plain furnishings. There was a kitchenette corner with small stove,
fridge and toaster, and on the other side of the room
a narrow single bed with a mosquito net suspended
above it. A thin sheet and blanket lay folded on the
bed. An old school desk held an antique telephone.

'You have the *en suite*.' Jonah pointed to the bowl
and jug of water for washing. 'Ladies' toilet is also
the men's room and is around the corner next to the
laundry. Knock firmly before you enter and if it's
empty lock the door when you're in there.'

'I'm sure I'll manage.' She tilted her head. 'What
makes it less dangerous here for you than for me,
apart from the fact that I'm a woman?'

'You mean apart from my time as a surgeon in the
army? Or the fact that I grew up here? Or the fact
that the boys don't fancy me? Gee, Dr McCloud, I
guess there's no reason I should be safer than you.'

She wondered how long he would continue the sar-
castic bite to his voice before he recovered from her
arrival. Jacinta compressed her lips and just nodded
politely as he spoke.

'Silly question.'

'That's right. I'll meet you at the top of the steps
of the hospital in ten minutes if you'd like to wash
and…' he glanced at her bare arms '…change.'
Jacinta only just managed to keep a rein on her

temper by reminding herself he would like to make her quit.

Exactly ten minutes later she stood outside the single-storied hospital front entrance with her arms safely covered in a long-sleeved shirt and suitably plastered with repellent.

Jonah was waiting. 'I'll take you in and introduce you around.'

They moved through the doors and she glanced up at the slowly rotating ceiling fans, surprised how cool it was inside the building as they walked across to a plain wooden desk at the head of the room that served as the nurse's desk. The woman seated there had by far the darkest skin Jacinta had seen and her hair was piled high on her head with a bone clasp.

'Dr Jacinta McCloud, this is Carla. Carla is the head nurse and will help you with your clinics.' Carla smiled shyly.

'Welcome, Doctor.'

Jacinta held out her hand and took the woman's capable fingers. 'It's nice to meet you, Carla.' Carla accompanied them as they moved down the room.

A teenage boy came in through a side door carrying a jug of water and Jonah stopped him. 'This is Jay. He's an orderly or, as they call them here, doctor boy.'

'Hello, Jay.' Jacinta smiled and the boy ducked his head shyly until they moved on.

A tall, blond-haired man in theatre scrubs bounded up the side steps and stopped beside them.

Jonah gestured with his hand. 'Dr Jacinta McCloud,

this tall streak of American dynamism is Dr Chuck Ford, who is here for four months and goes home next month. Chuck can't get enough of us.' Chuck grinned and held out his hand.

'Hi there, Jacinta. Welcome to Pudjip. It's a wild place.' He looked at Jonah. 'We've an early mark in Theatre today so I'm off to delivery to see what I can see.'

'Don't you love the enthusiasm of youth?' Jonah's comment was more under his breath than out loud, but Jacinta heard it and stored his cynicism for later to ponder. He turned back to her.

'The first week you'll practise the language working here in Pudjip while you conduct physical examinations, take histories and note symptoms. Most of it will be in pidgin English. Once you're more confident with the language it will be a lot easier for you.

'The difficult thing to accept here is that the choices for treatment at home are not obtainable here. You have to learn what's available and what's not for your treatment options. After that orientation you'll go on call here for a week to get some skills in treating the illnesses that are most common.' He paused.

She nodded that she understood and he went on. 'If you handle that OK you can accompany me on the next mission trip. Those trips last about ten days and we take a medical team to an outreach health centre. I gather your term is eight weeks?'

He shot her a look and Jacinta returned it calmly. 'Does that mean we're together for the next two months?' When he nodded with another one of those sardonic smiles she was careful to keep her face expressionless.

Great, she thought, attitude for weeks. But she'd asked for it. Jacinta glanced down the rows of mostly full beds. 'So how many patients have you in at the moment?'

If he was disappointed that she didn't comment on them being together for an extended time, he didn't show it. 'About eighty, but we had more than a hundred here during the chickenpox epidemic.'

One of the patients called out to Carla and she left the two doctors to complete the tour on their own.

'I hope I don't see an epidemic while I'm here,' Jacinta said.

'So do I,' he said soberly. 'We lose too many patients.'

Stricken, she stared at him, and at her distress he finally eased up on her. He ran his hand over the back of his head. 'Hang it, Jacinta, why did you come?'

'Because I can help?' she suggested quietly.

He rubbed his head again and she wondered if he had a headache. Probably from stewing over her arrival. The thought made her smile. So he was a grump, not a dictator, and she could forgive him that.

'Because I'm interested in tropical medicine and always have been. Because I do have something to offer and the time and money to spare to make it happen. Do you have the right to turn that kind of help away?' This was the crux of the matter.

'No, I don't. We do need people like you and I

guess you'll come to realise that this place is more than some big adventure. I just, personally, wish you hadn't come.'

'Gee, thanks. That was the impression I got at the airstrip.'

He laughed without amusement. 'Impressions can be deceptive. If I was in Sydney I'd be delighted to see you. You're not hard on the eye.'

She suppressed her smile. 'Good grief. Was that a back-handed compliment, Dr Armstrong? I may faint.'

'Not until your days off, Doctor.' But this time he smiled.

Jonah drank in the sight of her. He couldn't help himself. It wasn't his problem if she decided she could handle this place and take care of herself. But if anything happened to her, he knew it would be his concern no matter what she or he said, and that was what he was afraid of.

Her tailored trousers and long-sleeved top were loose enough to keep her cool but fitted enough to let him know there was a very desirable woman under those clothes. And that was the meat of the problem. He found her very desirable.

She'd probably bought her clothes through some yuppie traveller's mail-order site because, though they were appropriate, they just shrieked money and style. The whims of the rich. He hoped no miscreant decided she was worth a good ransom.

How she would cope with the primitive conditions was yet to be seen, but he had to admit she hadn't

commented on anything so far as being unsatis-
factory.

Her dark hair was confined in a tight bun to keep
her cool in the heat, but it left the lovely curve of her
neck so softly vulnerable he wanted to put a scarf on
her. And the way she kept raising those extraordinary
brows at him every time he barked at her, he was
hard put not to smile.

He'd have to be extra careful he didn't get used to
having her around because she was only here for eight
weeks.

On the good side, it could prove to be an interesting
two months, as long as he could keep her safe from
the dangers in PNG and the bigger danger of himself.

The next few days were unlike anything Jacinta had
expected. Despite her attempt to study the language
prior to her trip, the dialects of the visiting sick kept
changing and it was slow going, learning pidgin
English. But she persevered.

By the fifth day she could pick up most of the
important information her patients wanted to convey
to her, but there were healthy doses of hand motions
included.

After a particularly frustrating half-hour trying to
understand an elderly woman with abdominal pain,
she'd had to call Jonah. In one short sharp sentence
he discovered the woman thought she'd swallowed a
chicken bone that she could feel in her stomach.

'I can't believe that was what she was trying
to say.'

'You have to understand that English is spoken by only one to two per cent of the inhabitants. Pidgin is widespread but there are seven hundred and fifteen indigenous languages to mix with it. You can imagine the struggle for the ruling government to be understood by even half the people.'

Then she didn't feel so bad, especially when he added, 'You're doing remarkably well.' Praise from Jonah was sparse, and she hugged the grain to herself to pull out later that night in her lonely room.

Six hours later, when the clinical day was complete, the medical staff had met and eaten supper and the lights were being extinguished all over the station. Jacinta leaned on the doorframe of her room and pondered how in some ways the village wasn't as primitive as she'd feared.

There was a telephone and internet connection now that Jonah set up an account for her, so she could at least e-mail Noni and her father when the phone lines were working, which they sometimes did.

In other ways it was more primitive than she had ever imagined. To the PNG nationals, death by illness and violence and accident were sad facts of life, and the lack of medical supplies ensured that she would never take for granted her facilities in Sydney when she went home.

To Jacinta's surprise she'd felt a kinship with the people she'd met. She delighted in the shy smiles and singing as the women worked, the happy children—both PNG nationals and missionary kids that played so well together, and the bright clothes worn.

And she wept inside for the stoic acceptance when illnesses that had brought patients to the mission hospital had taken too great a hold to be cured.

'You shouldn't be outside in the dark!' Jonah's voice made her heart trip and she snapped her head around.

'I didn't hear you come across the gravel.'

'I'm an elephant compared to some of the locals, which is why you shouldn't be out here alone after dark. You should stay locked in your room.'

CHAPTER FOUR

JONAH was genuinely upset and in the few days she'd been there she'd heard enough gruesome stories to accept he was only concerned for her safety. She hated being in the wrong.

'I'm sorry.' She stepped back into her doorway. 'You're right, but it was such a beautiful night after this afternoon's rain I needed to feel the air. Are you going for a walk?'

Jacinta could hear the wistfulness in her own voice and she suspected he did, too, because he sighed.

'Only a short one, but you can come if you wish.' His tone wasn't as welcoming as she'd have liked but the lure of some time outside the hut was too attractive to be picky. She slipped back inside to grab her light cardigan, and to her surprise he took her hand as they began to walk.

'You are a confusing man, Jonah Armstrong,' she muttered, and she shook their clasped hands to illustrate her point.

He looked down at their entwined fingers. 'This is just to stop you wandering off.' He squeezed her fingers and she hugged the warmth of even that tiny movement to herself.

He went on. 'At least I have some control over the danger, if I can pull you back out of the way.' There

59

was laughter in his voice and she could feel the spread of euphoria that they were regaining some of the banter she remembered from Sydney.

'And I thought you just wanted to hold my hand.'

'That, too,' he said, as if them doing so was the most natural thing in the world. She was plunged back into confusion.

She didn't understand this man and it terrified her the way he could rouse her emotions with a word or two and a quick squeeze of her fingers. Was he aware or was it just her? 'Why would you want to hold my hand?'

'It's a nice hand,' he said. He lifted her fingers to his face and squinted at them in the dim light and then placed her palm between both of his. 'You have slim fingers, fingernails not too long, a little rough at the edges from constant washing, like all of us, but the whole hand fits nicely in mine.' He pulled her hand back to his side and they continued walking. The air seemed to vibrate between them.

She felt a little breathless and struggled to keep the conversation light. 'Thank you, kind sir, for the potted description of my hand.'

Jacinta could feel the pull of attraction and the frivolous conversation was nowhere near the depth of feeling that was running between them. The scent of soap from his shower drifted towards her every now and then as they walked, and the deliberate crunch of his footsteps, so much heavier than hers, made her aware of his strength. He laughed and she closed her eyes briefly at the warmth in that sound.

'You are such a prickly woman,' he murmured.

Jacinta exhaled noisily. 'You confuse me and I find that hard to cope with.'

'That's another thing I like so much about you, Jacinta. Your honesty is refreshing.'

His comment made her feel uncomfortable because there was so much he didn't know about her. She changed the subject. 'Did you buy the house we looked at?'

He laughed. 'Yes, I did. My solicitor e-mailed me yesterday to say the sale was through. So I now have the first official home I can remember.'

'Are you glad?'

He shrugged. 'It feels strange to be a home-owner. Maybe I'm growing up.'

She laughed. 'Don't grow much more or you won't fit through the doorways.'

'Does my height bother you?'

The comment came out of the dark before she could stop it. 'Kiss me and I'll tell you.'

'Don't mind if I do,' he said, and she knew then he had been feeling the build-up of tension, too.

His face came closer and their lips touched gently as she reached up to put her hands around his neck. When she slid her fingers up and over his shoulders his taut muscles felt like corded steel beneath his shirt, and she curved her fingers into his neck with a sigh as the kiss deepened.

He slid his hands down her back and cupped her bottom so that he could lift her slightly towards him. Jacinta wasn't sure if it was the loss of the ground beneath her feet or the sudden depth of his kiss that made her feel as though she was flying. Either way, she didn't want Jonah to stop.

For Jonah it was everything he'd feared. He suppressed a groan at the sweetness she offered him, but in his heart he'd known it would be like this. He'd known from the first moment he'd opened his eyes at Pickford that she would be a danger to everything he thought he had control over.

The kiss waxed and waned and waxed, and his stomach kicked with every stroke of her mouth against his. Every nuance of movement burned like a furnace against him and he could feel the control slipping from his fingers like silk.

They had to stop. Slowly he pulled back, lowered her feet to the ground and released her. She swayed slightly in his arms as if she would fall. His grip tightened until she steadied and, as much as he didn't want to, he put her away from him.

Her voice was dreamy as she continued to sway a little. 'Your height doesn't bother me.'

He looked at her flushed face in the moonlight and fought against his desire to pull her back into his arms. He had no idea what she was talking about. His mind was fogged with his urge to pick her up and carry her back to his hut and all the reasons he couldn't. He struggled to find something to say.

'I admire the way you've coped with our primitive conditions.'

She pulled her hand free and put more distance between them. 'What?'

'I think you've fitted in really well here, especially when you're used to the high life.'

She screwed up her face and stared at him. 'Don't patronise me, Jonah. You know nothing of my life, so don't prejudge through ignorance.'

Jonah stopped and turned to look at her. He'd upset her and it was a measure of the imbalance she caused him that he'd done so. But maybe it was better that distance had been established between them again.

'I apologise.' He cast a brief look towards the stars as if for inspiration on not compounding his mistake. 'So tell me, Jacinta, why do you manage so well?'

She looked up at him and lowered her brows, and he realised she was trying to see if he meant what he'd said.

Had he been that hard on her? 'I'm serious. I'd like to know.'

They started to walk again and he took back her hand. After some initial resistance she let him.

The warmth of her fingers in his did strange things to his heart, and so did her next words.

'My mother was a single parent and we only scraped through as well as we did because she refused to be beaten. I admired her greatly.'

'It must have been hard for you.'

'It was harder for her but she chose not to tell my father of my existence.'

Jacinta's voice came out of the dimness beside him. 'When she died I ran away from the man she lived with and ended up in squatters' digs and conditions that weren't much different to these.' She lifted her hand to include the camp. 'And in some ways much worse than here.'

'How old were you?'

'Sixteen.' He shuddered and couldn't imagine what it must have been like for her.

Her voice dropped and he had to strain to catch her next words. 'I became pregnant from a doomed relationship, then my father found out about me and took me in for the last two months of my pregnancy.'

'Was it hard to get to know him?'

'Sure. It took me a long time to trust that he wouldn't decide that he didn't want me again. That was what I'd learnt. Men would let you down if you relied on them. So it was better to make do, and not wait for the time they would let you down.'

There was a smile in her voice when she spoke again. 'My father was very patient with the surly teenager I'd become, supported me when things were tough until I could stand on my own two feet. Noni and Dad were there for me...' Her voice dropped even further. 'When my baby died.' She lifted her chin. 'But now they have their own lives and I have mine.'

His heart contracted and he realised that he who dealt with death and illness every day could scarcely bear the thought of Jacinta's suffering. 'I'm so sorry. How did your baby die?'

She kept her chin up. 'Olivia had a congenital heart defect that couldn't be repaired. She was four weeks old when she died, but she touched all our lives with beauty and strength that I'll never forget.'

He could only imagine the pain such a loss would cause to a mother. All he could go on were the feelings he'd been left with after Melinda had died. He wanted to hug Jacinta close in sympathy—take her pain and protect her from ever feeling such agony again. But he could no more protect her from that than he could promise to keep her safe here.

Then she did something strange. She stopped and turned her ankle and he looked down to see what she was pointing to. 'This is my butterfly.' There was a tiny gold and green winged figure tattooed on her ankle. He wasn't a fan of tattoos but this one touched him in a way he didn't understand.

Her voice went on softly, 'In memory of my daughter, Olivia—just like your butterfly…' she touched the ring on his finger '…is in memory of your sister.'

All the old fears and horror from when Melinda had disappeared loomed over him, and he wished uselessly and with all his heart that Jacinta were safely back in Sydney.

And he wished she hadn't told him because now he felt even closer to her. They'd both been shaped by tragedy in their past and he didn't doubt that she was stronger from the loss of her daughter. He could feel himself drawn more and more under her spell every second, and that wasn't good.

When she was at work, settled into routine, she fitted in so beautifully his misgivings had doubled. The challenge of maintaining his distance from her was undermining his good intentions. His admiration of how well she coped with the workload and the environment was part of it, but the fact that he was so aware of her presence unsettled him no matter what she was doing.

He could pick Jacinta's quiet voice out above others and recognise her soft laughter in a roomful of people. The cadence of her voice coming from the darkness beside him as they walked reminded him of his first memories of her and made him long to do all the things sleep allowed him to dream of at night alone in his bed.

His voice was very quiet and deep. 'Let's stop talking and listen to the night.' He turned his face up to the stars. They were silent for a few minutes. 'This is what I miss in the cities—the sounds of the night.'

She wondered at his thoughts, and the conflicting messages she was receiving, and she wondered why she'd told him more than she'd told anyone except her father and Noni. She concentrated on listening to the constant buzz and hum and tick of the insects and frogs.

Alone, she would have been uneasy with the rustle of undergrowth from unseen animals and the call of some raucous bird, but with Jonah beside her it all combined to create an orchestra of living but invisible inhabitants of the bush.

As she savoured how alive the night was, the moon shone from behind the leaves of a huge tree and clouds skittered across in front of it, dimming and brightening their path.

'It's beautiful,' she sighed. His hand tightened.

He didn't say anything for a few minutes and then he said, 'Yes, it is. And dangerous.'

He dropped her fingers and she felt suddenly rudderless in the dark. 'And so are you. That's what frightens me.' The ring on his finger glinted as he raised his hand to run his fingers through his hair.

The stern inflection from Mt Hagen airport was back in his voice when he spoke next. 'Please, remember that it is not recommended for women to walk in the station at night on their own or walk off the station outside the gates at any time.'

She wished he'd let it rest. 'You're labouring the point.' He was spoiling the mood.

Then he totally destroyed it. 'I knew someone who never came back. She broke the rule. I don't want that to happen to you.'

The next morning as the sun rose a young native woman was carried in on a makeshift stretcher by grieving relatives. Abducted by the young tribal men, she'd suffered horrific burns and had been near death when her family had found her.

Jonah and Carla helped bandage the victim and give intravenous fluids, even though they knew they couldn't save her. At least morphine could lighten some of her pain.

When the young woman passed away just before lunchtime, Jacinta could feel the splintering of horror inside herself and the black ball of revenge lodged in her chest as she wished she could find those responsible.

'Don't go there, Jacinta.' Jonah had come up behind her.

She stood on the back veranda of the hospital and her fingernails dug into a post in helpless rage. She shuddered when his fingers traced the tears down her cheek and he shook his head as he pulled her into his chest for comfort. Then his arms came around her and she began to sob.

He allowed her to do so for a few moments and he stroked her hair before he spoke. 'They are not of your world. Rebel crime may have heavily decreased in recent years, yet there can be isolated instances and they can be horrific. But if what people do is wrong, like today, then their own laws will catch up with them. There is darkness here but there is also the most beautiful spirit within these people.'

She lifted her eyes to his. 'You really believe that the beauty outweighs the bad?'

He shrugged. 'I have to. Because what we do matters, and I'm not willing to walk away from the good because of the bad.'

She sniffed and drew in a shaking breath as she dried her eyes on her sleeve. 'Their behaviour puts a different light on my adventure.'

He smiled and hugged her close once more before he let her go. 'Is this where I get to tell you I told you so?' She stiffened and he smiled again. 'Your heart's in the right place. Here, you learn to grow up fast. On bad days I feel so bent over with the weight of what I can't do I forget what we are achieving, and that is when I begin to straighten again.

'Things have greatly improved since the civil war ended. But I grew up with this life—I can't imagine how challenging it would be for someone from a different life to watch helplessly as things like this happen.

'A wise man said of our work, "We are hardpressed but nowhere near hopeless."' He turned her around and pushed her towards the door. 'I remember that when I feel like you do now.'

He gave her a little push. 'You need to put an IV cannula in little Peeta. His chemotherapy is due and he doesn't cry when you do it. Then we must make the round of patients we didn't have time for this morning.'

Work did help. The day remained sober but there were moments when she was reminded that they did comfort those who needed them.

Peeta, at five, had been diagnosed with leukaemia. The chemotherapy did help and his prognosis was improving. One of the first people Jacinta had seen, Peeta had been almost dead on her first day. Five days later he was eating and had even managed a laugh at Jacinta's appalling pidgin attempt to tell him a joke.

When she went back inside he was standing beside his bed, waiting for her, and she hurried over.

She tilted her head questionly, smiled and pointed to the bed to ask why he was up.

'Me canna.'

Jacinta smiled and bent down to hug the little boy. 'That's right. You can. You are growing so strong. You so clebber.' As she knelt, with his dark head under her chin, she realised what Jonah meant. They *were* helping and they *were* needed.

For the rest of the day she seemed more aware of what Jonah did in his spare moments. Those he could help with surgery he operated on swiftly and decisively, and those who were beyond the surgeon's knife he spent more time with, sitting on their beds for a minute or two every time he passed.

And he passed often because he was everywhere.

The morning clinic they'd missed was moved to the afternoon and they saw sixty patients before a late afternoon tea.

All three doctors barely stopped and the nurses— all Papuans—worked tirelessly towards the smooth running of the hospital. Jacinta couldn't help comparing it to Pickford's where adherence to teabreaks was a priority for Administration.

She felt marooned outside her body all of that day, watching what went on and helping where she could, yet always aware of Jonah as he worked, as she believed he was aware of her. It was almost as if he sensed her need to be linked to someone who knew where she came from and how she thought.

By the end of the day she was mentally as well as physically exhausted and slipped away to her room to lie on her bed. She stared at the six-inch lizard that crawled up the wall in her bedroom and wished she'd never come. She wanted her father and Noni, her safe house and to never think of this place again. But even if she'd had the first two she knew the third would never happen.

Jonah recognised her dilemma. It was common for the volunteers to have sudden bouts of homesickness, especially after such a graphic example of how different this world was from the one they were used to. And he was more in tune with this volunteer than he'd ever been before.

When he knocked on her screen door she was slow to open it, and he wondered for a moment if she was asleep, but when he saw her face he knew.

'May I come in?' Her eyes flickered with surprise and then she stood back to allow him to enter. She remained standing in the centre of the room and kept her gaze on her hands.

'Let me guess.' He smiled and stepped up to her, and with a gentle finger he tilted her chin so he could see her eyes. 'You'd like a magic carpet that would pop you safely in your bed in Sydney away from all the horrible things you've seen here.'

'Yes.' Her voice was small and her eyes were shadowed. Unable to help himself, he bent his head and brushed her lips with his own. That same sweetness was there and he dared not dwell on it. 'These feelings will pass and then you'll go on, stronger and more determined to not be cast down by outside influences.'

'But what if I'm not strong enough?'

He pulled her face into his chest and hugged her. 'I can see your strength. You are one of the strongest women I know. You just haven't tested yourself lately. Be gentle and it will come.'

He put her away from him and stepped back because suddenly he wanted to do more than just kiss her lightly on the lips. And Pudjip was not the place for liaisons.

With a woman like Jacinta it would be no light fling. She was no woman he could walk away from. An affair with her would be like a tropical cyclone and the strength of it would change the countryside of their lives for ever.

If he accepted she was inside his heart, he would never survive if anything happened to her. He'd made that pact many years ago and he couldn't afford to change that now, but she needed a break.

'I'll see you in the morning. After clinic, I thought we might take a drive to the local market. You haven't seen much of the fun side and it's only a week until we leave for the Sepik. You could brush up on your pidgin.'

Jacinta watched him let himself out with mixed feelings. She followed him to the door and locked it after him because she knew he would listen to check that she did.

He'd offered her a treat like a homesick child. That was how he thought of her. For a moment there she'd hoped he was going to crush her to him, and she'd felt her body lean towards his. The irony was that he'd missed it. It wasn't to be.

She was just one of the volunteers who came and went for a week or a month or a few months, and life would go on after she went home. He'd pushed her away. Gently, it was true, but without any room for misunderstandings. What the heck was she doing here?

The next morning the sun rose on another glorious day and Jacinta smiled her way through the ward rounds with Jonah and then the outpatient clinic. She really did need to remember that she was here for the medical experience. Jonah was just a mostly friendly face in her environment.

Driving to the market, it was harder to remember that. The sun shone through the window of the Jeep onto his hands as he capably manoeuvred the vehicle around the bends, and she remembered the strength and comfort from those same hands when he'd held her.

He turned his head and said something she didn't catch then laughed. His eyes crinkled at the corners and his beautiful mouth softened with delight, and the sight pierced her heart with regret.

'I'm sorry. I missed that,' she said, but really she wanted him to smile like that again and warm the chilled areas she couldn't seem to warm in her soul. He didn't oblige but how could he know her need? She didn't understand it herself.

'What's wrong, Jacinta? You've been very quiet this morning. Is the tragedy of yesterday still playing on your mind?'

'I think so.' It was easier to say yes than to say, When you kissed me is on my mind, because I think I'm falling in love with you. She blinked and hurriedly turned her head to look sightlessly out of the window. Her mouth dried and a flare of panic fluttered in her stomach. It wasn't true. Couldn't be true.

The thought had flashed into her mind and she tried desperately to erase the memory of considering such a thing, but the echoes of the idea wouldn't go away. The scenery flashed past the window and even the produce-laden locals walking the beaten road towards the market were unseen by her.

Impossible relationship. That was all they could ever have. There was no future for them, with Jonah living only for Pudjip and refusing to consider a wife or family placed at risk here. She had her own family and her own full life in Sydney, and she could never leave all that she had achieved and place herself under the control of any man. Even Jonah.

'So tell me about the markets. Are they big? How much further is it?' She was babbling but he didn't seem to notice.

'If you're thinking Paddy's Markets in Sydney, it's nothing like that. Where we're going, the women gather in the centre of the village and trade their handicrafts and food while the men gossip. You have to haggle for a bargain or they'll be disappointed.'

He looked across at her. 'Do you have any money on you?'

She nodded, still in shock from her thoughts but more sure she could control her wayward feelings. The quicker they arrived at some distraction, the better.

The village was tiny, but the huts were circular and well made and the view across the mountains was spectacular. Vibrant green foliage came within a few feet of the edge of the village. The dirt road ran through the centre and dozens of colourful locals were raucously gathered as they bartered.

The bright feathers and headscarves of the men and women stood out in the dark-skinned crowd and the sun beat down on Jacinta's hair as she climbed out of the car. This was different and exciting and free from tragedy, and she was glad she'd come.

Children swerved in and out of the crowd, laughing and skipping with excitement, and when they saw Jonah they crowded around, grinning at him and pulling on his hands.

He laughed and as she watched he picked up a little girl of about five and hugged her and then swung her around to face Jacinta. 'This is Genna. Say hello to Missy-Dokkta.'

Genna tucked her face into Jonah's shoulder and giggled. 'Genna had a ruptured appendix and we had to fight to save her.' He hugged her again. 'But she's fighter.' He put the little girl down, pulled some sweets from his pocket and proceeded to call each of the children by name. He pointed to Jacinta.

'Missy-Dokkta come look see.'

'Hello, Dokkta,' they chorused and crowded around her, and suddenly she was being pulled towards the market area in a group of laughing children. She looked back over her shoulder at Jonah and he was smiling with an expression in his eyes she hadn't seen before.

When the children left her, she wandered up and

down the row of vendors and admired the handicrafts the women had created. She bought three beautiful string bags in greens and gold that the native women filled with produce and strapped to their foreheads to keep their hands free. One was for Noni, one for her stepsister Nanette and one for herself. Jacinta slid the strap around her head and carried her purchases that way, too.

As a means of carrying things, the bag was remarkably comfortable. She bought two small Hagen masks, one in a dark wood with shells for eyes for her father and one hand-painted in ochres which she thought Noni's son Harley might like.

Tucked away on a carpet, a lovely carved pot, intricately painted and made out of a coconut, drew Jacinta's attention. It had a tiny fitted lid and she admired the object several times but she couldn't decide whether to buy it.

'Do you fancy that?' Jonah appeared behind her and he draped an arm over her shoulder. 'You'll start rumours with that one.'

She smiled up at him and guiltily savoured the teasing note in his voice and the weight of his arm on her shoulder. 'What is it?'

'It's a fertility gourd. The witchdoctor fills it with magic herbs for a price to make a fertility potion.'

She laughed at him. 'Do you believe in that?'

'Of course not.' He picked it up and admired it. 'It's very pretty, though.' He turned to the toothless old women who'd made it and matched the wicked

grin on her face with one of his own. 'I'll take it,' he
said in pidgin.

He handed it to Jacinta with a flourish and laughed
at her confusion. Then he left her to talk to a tall
native with a wooden leg, and she could hear his
laugh ring out with something the man said to him.

They left not long after that and Jacinta watched
the spectacular greens of the foliage blur past her window. It had been good to get away for the morning
and she knew she would savour these memories
shared with Jonah.

'Did you enjoy that?' Jonah asked indulgently.

'Very much.' She smiled at him. 'You're very pop-
ular with the children.'

'Children have good taste.'

'Ha! I always knew you were conceited. I saw you
bribe them.' He laughed and she became quiet as they
drove. Jonah Armstrong would be a hard man to forget.

The next morning Jonah was his normal bossy self.
Just after rounds began, a call came through for help
in the delivery room where an older mother was in
the final stages of labour. When they arrived, the
mother's water had broken and the tiny buttocks of
her baby were sitting curled on his mother's perineum
as if testing the waters outside his haven.

Jacinta's eyes widened and Jonah whistled before
moving over to the scrub sink. 'The best thing with
a breech is to leave well alone,' he said over his
shoulder. 'Pop your gloves on and I'll guide you.

Most of the time a breech baby will sort itself out. You should do this delivery in case you're on your own one day.'

Jacinta hesitated. 'I've only done my obstetric rotation in my training. I didn't specialise in obstetrics.'

He grinned. 'Neither did I, but we haven't got an obstetrician here today.'

Jacinta nodded and swallowed the feeling of trepidation in her throat, but Jonah's words appeared prophetic. The baby's body gradually appeared with the help of gravity and his mother's efforts. Soon the baby's hips descended and it became apparent there was a new male in the family as a tiny scrotum swung into view.

As they prepared for the birth, first one and then the other of the baby's legs dropped down so that the waist and a stretched part of the umbilical cord appeared.

'You could ease a loop of cord out to save strain on it, but I like to leave it in case I cause spasm in the cord.' Jonah spoke softly at her shoulder and she watched a section of the slippery rope slip out of the birth canal. All Jacinta needed to do was rest her hand under the baby's belly and wait.

'Makes sense,' she said. In fact, it all made sense and her exhilaration mounted.

Jonah went on softly, 'Make sure you keep the spine upwards. If the presenting part looks like rotating to belly up, you need to keep gentle traction on the baby's pelvis by holding the upper legs with your curled fingers and resting your thumbs on the dimples of the pelvis. That prevents you from squeezing any abdominal organs if you got excited and tried to pull.'

'I promise I won't try to pull.' Jacinta slipped her fingers into position as Jonah had instructed, and he laughed softly.

'Never doubted it,' he said. 'That's where people get into trouble, though, by pulling before the umbilicus descends, because it makes the baby extend his head or pop an arm up. That's the last thing you want.'

The baby's trunk delivered quickly and Jacinta allowed the infant to rotate slightly to the left as the natural curves of the mother's pelvis facilitated delivery of first one shoulder and arm and then rotated the other way so that the other arm came free.

Finally only the baby's head remained to be born.

She glanced across at Jonah, who nodded and demonstrated in the air how she should support the baby and allow the baby to rest on her forearm until the nape of the neck appeared.

'Breech babies really don't have a long time to mould their heads through the pelvis and I like to slow delivery of the head for that reason. Put your fingers like this.'

Jonah encouraged one of her hands under the baby's face to place one of her fingertips on each side of the little boy's cheekbones and with her other hand have fingers spread over shoulders and nape of his neck to prevent his head from being born too quickly.

'What's next?' Jonah prompted.

'Now we can lift his legs up slowly and the face

will be born by the baby slowly lifting his chin as his head goes through the pelvis.' The baby did as they expected and suddenly it was over.

'My first breech delivery,' she whispered, as she laid the baby on his mother's stomach.

Jonah looked on but then his eyes widened and a slow smile spread across his face. 'Don't go away because the second one is about to come.'

The second twin was also a frank breech and again two little buttocks presented and another little scrotum. Jacinta couldn't help a tiny laugh as again the procedure was accomplished easily. 'So why do we do so many Caesareans for breech presentation in Australia?'

'Because here the mothers come to hospital a lot later in labour than they do in Pickford.'

Jacinta delivered the second placenta and Jonah was quick to massage the mother's stomach. The idea was to encourage the placental site on her uterus to clamp down to prevent haemorrhage.

He asked a question of the mother and she answered in heavy pidgin that Jacinta couldn't follow. 'Kea has only been here for fifteen minutes because she walked from twenty miles away.'

Jacinta's mouth dropped open and she laughed. 'That's one way to keep off the bed in labour.'

Both babies were close to five pounds and the mother didn't seem perturbed that there were two. 'Kea has had twins before so she'll probably go home tomorrow. I doubt the babies will have problems. This

is her ninth pregnancy, so I'm more worried that she
will bleed.'

He spoke to both the nurse and Kea and nodded
encouragingly as both babies were put to the breast.
'Hopefully an early breastfeed by these guys will release more oxytocin and keep her uterus well contracted.'

When Jacinta had washed, Jonah gave last instruc-
tions to the nurse and they returned to the other side
of the hospital. They didn't make it to the wards.

Intercepted by the emergency department nurse,
Jonah took off at a trot and Jacinta, who hadn't understood the message, followed him. When they arrived, the ward was filled with people, many circling
aimlessly with bloodied hands and heads and broken
limbs.

A utility truck had overturned going up a mountain,
and the men riding in the back had been tipped onto
the road. Luckily nobody had been killed but the
noise was horrendous as the victims tried to make
themselves heard.

With a short, sharp command Jonah silenced the
majority of the voices and gestured to Jacinta to move
to his side.

'Triage them, will you? I'll start here because this
fellow needs a chest drain for a pneumothorax, but
the others seem stable. Make sure Nurse hasn't
missed anything major.'

The next two hours saw a procession of patients
pass through the X-ray department as Jacinta splinted
and padded wounds until she could get around to su-

turing those that needed it. Only one young man required an anaesthetic while the others were stitched and plastered in the emergency ward and then discharged.

Jacinta and Jonah looked at each other as the last man departed, and both smiled. 'Now, that was a little more like a Monday morning in Pickford,' she said as she stripped off her gloves.

'You're even getting better with your pidgin. I think you'll enjoy the change when we go on our field surgery.'

Jonah wondered if he was going to enjoy it. Usually he relished the trek, but this time he knew he'd be conscious of Jacinta every step of the way. At least here in the hospital he could keep her safe in the compound and get away from her if he found himself spending too much time watching her.

On the trek they'd be together from necessity, and he'd be watching her for other reasons. He wondered if it was too late to change plans.

'What are you thinking?'

Her voice broke into his thoughts and he didn't meet her eyes. 'About the trip next week.'

'You looked very grim,' she said.

He rubbed the back of his neck. He'd known she was tenacious. 'I'm wondering if perhaps it would be better if you stayed here.'

Jacinta lifted her head. 'I thought we'd agreed I was going with you.' The light of battle in her eyes was clear and he marvelled at the difference from the shattered woman of two nights ago.

'It will be no picnic. And as well as possible threat from the locals, however rare, it's an insect and wild animal fest that makes this place look like a five-star hotel.'

She glared at him and he had to suppress a smile at her ferocity. 'If I'd wanted a five-star hotel I would have stayed in Sydney. Tell me about the Sepik.'

'The Sepik.' The memories filled his mind and he could almost smell the heavy river odours and feel the dampness of the river air on his skin.

'There's nowhere like it. As you know, it's to the north of us and covers an extensive area. The rivers wind through the jungle and huge tracts of marshes and crocodile-infested lowlands provide a home for snakes and aggressive wild pigs.'

Her eyebrows lifted and she murmured, 'Snakes? I may be from Australia, but I still hate them.'

He grinned, glad to find something she couldn't romanticise. 'Snakes!'

He went on, 'The villages hug the shoreline and the houses are built on stilts to accommodate the rise and fall of the river. The thing I remember most is the number of canoes. All sizes, from one for the smallest child to larger family craft, all tied below each house to stakes. And it's stinking hot and the mosquitoes are vicious. I think that's where I picked up my dose of malaria from last time.'

'I'm covered and I'll be careful. What about the clinics?'

'The clinics are crowded. People travel for days to see the doctors and the equipment we have is never extensive enough to cover all the needs. But some we can help and it's those successes that drag me back every time.'

'You need me with you.' She said it quietly and they both knew it was true.

He weakened, as he'd feared he would. 'I know.' But he sighed. 'I'll have to leave the arrangements as they are. I'm going back to check on Kea, you go on to lunch and I'll see you soon.'

She nodded and he watched her walk away. She was occupying more of his thoughts each day, especially since he'd kissed her, and he needed more control. The trouble was, every time he deliberately set up distance between them something happened and he found her in his arms. It was funny how the other doctors didn't end up there, he thought cynically.

Jonah shook his head and turned left towards the delivery rooms. Just over six weeks until she was gone.

CHAPTER FIVE

THE morning they left Pudjip it was sunny and the breeze was light as they drove the winding Highland Highway to Mt Hagen at a clipping pace.

The Missionary Air Fellowship plane would fly the team to Wewak and then onto Hauna village, where they would take dugout canoes filled with equipment up the jungle-bordered Sepik River.

Jonah and Jacinta were accompanied by Carla and her husband Samuel, the anaesthetic nurse, and they were to meet another missionary couple, Bob and Marsha Giles. Bob's specialty was ENT—ears, nose and throat—and Marsha was a paediatrician. They made the trip every year from New York.

Like Jonah, they knew the dangers but also the rewards.

An hour outside Hagen, in one of the more desolate spots, they found the road blocked by a fallen tree. Jonah slowed the vehicle and when they stopped both he and Samuel appeared reluctant to leave the four-wheel drive and tackle the obstacle.

Jacinta turned from one to the other, confused by the mixed signals and tension that had suddenly filled the vehicle.

'No heroics, Samuel,' Jonah ordered out of the side of his mouth, and she thought that a strange comment until four tribesmen appeared out of the jungle. Jonah put the car in reverse, but before they could turn the vehicle another four men appeared to surround it.

The leader gestured to Jonah, who opened his door and climbed out. Samuel did the same.

'Stay in the car,' he said to the women, and Carla nodded as she watched the renegades circle both men.

The leader and Jonah struck up a spirited discussion, and judging by the vigorous negative from Jonah he didn't agree with the new plans.

When the natives raised their axes towards the women in the car, Jonah fell silent and put his hand out to stop Samuel from flinging himself on the raiders.

The icy trickle of dread settled in Jacinta's stomach when she heard Jonah make his decision. 'I'll go with them. Get in the car, Samuel.'

Samuel shook his head and one of the men stepped forward and hit the side of Samuel's head with the flat of his axe as an incentive to comply.

Samuel slid bonelessly to the ground and before Jonah could move there was a sharpened spear under his throat to prevent him interfering.

Helplessly he watched as Carla screamed and sprang from the car to her husband's side. Jacinta slid across the seat to help Carla, and the two women dragged the semi-conscious man into the back seat of the Land Rover.

Jonah called across the noise to Jacinta, 'Drive back to Pudjip. Chuck will know who to contact.'

The headman gestured at Jacinta, and Jonah vehemently shook his head, but the other man wouldn't give in. Two of the younger tribesmen approached the car with their spears and gestured for her to get out.

Jonah's face lacked any expression. There was nothing they could do to prevent her being taken, and a great risk in resistance.

'They say if you don't come they will kill Carla and Samuel. Someone knows you're a doctor, too, and they say they will let us go as soon as we have done what they ask. Bring what medical gear we can carry and send Carla and Samuel back to the hospital.'

Jacinta balled her fists to stop her hands from shaking and struggled to clear her mind as she gathered two small medical kits from the large amount they'd planned to take to the Sepik. As an afterthought she tossed in their personal antimalarials and water-purifying tablets.

The men with spears gestured for her to hurry, and she zipped up the bags and made her way over to Jonah. As soon as the two prisoners were together the party moved off in single file into the jungle. Jacinta couldn't believe what had just happened.

Jonah was behind her and his voice was reassuring. 'It should be OK. One of their people is sick but he's wanted by the authorities and they don't want to risk him being caught at the hospital.'

'Won't kidnapping us cause more of a police presence?'

'I wish,' he said dryly. 'Not for a while. Things move slowly up here. Unless they kill us.'

He went on, 'It hasn't happened in the past six years, but the usual scenario is that our mission will negotiate for our release. The best solution is that we save the patient, they send us back, the mission will have an apology from the tribe and we'll all pretend to be good friends again.'

She couldn't believe he was so calm. 'Has this happened to you before?'

'Twice.'

'No wonder you didn't want me to come.'

'Der.' His childish response made Jacinta's lips twitch, and she decided that if Jonah could make light of their situation then so could she. Or at least she could pretend to.

The men weren't angry or needlessly cruel towards her, but their tolerance was non-existent. If she slowed for any reason then the point of a spear would leave her in no doubt that she needed to move faster.

After half an hour she was finding it difficult to keep up the pace. She heard Jonah speak to one of their captors and her pack was taken and handed to Jonah. Despite her reluctance to doubly burden him, she sighed with relief.

'Thank you,' she muttered over her shoulder, and her mouth was so dry she croaked a little.

'We'll stop soon because there's a ravine we have to cross. Don't look down when we cross the rope bridge and watch out for vines or you'll trip. There's a waterfall not much further after that.'

'Do you know the place we're going to?'

'I've a fair idea for the first hour, but after that it will be new territory.'

'How long do you think it will be?'

'No idea. When we get there they'll let you rest. Keep your head down and don't aggravate them. Though if you get a good chance to escape, take it, and don't worry about me. It will be easier to escape one at a time than together. Don't even think about me because I'll be fine.'

Jacinta listened to his words but she never thought she'd act on them. The thought of being out here on her own gave her no comfort.

When they arrived at the camp it was easy to see the tribe weren't planning on staying long. There were about a dozen ragged tents and leantos made out of tarpaulins pegged to the ground around centre poles, a few straggling chickens, two fire pits and a huddle of women peeling some kind of root vegetable on the outskirts.

Jonah, carrying the medical supplies, was taken to the chief and Jacinta found herself pushed inside an empty tent. She could see the legs of the guard outside the entrance and stifled a half-hysterical laugh. She doubted she needed watching as she wasn't planning on walking off anywhere!

With her back against the central support, Jacinta slid down the shaft of the roughly hewn wood and settled her bottom on the ground to rest her shaking legs. She shut her eyes.

Images of Jonah being beaten or killed crowded her

mind, but she kept telling herself that Jonah had been in this kind of situation before. She didn't dare think about being left alone with the tribesmen if anything happened to Jonah.

Her thoughts made for a fitful rest but she must have dozed off because the light seemed different when she woke at Jonah's entrance. Thank God he was safe.

His face lit up with relief when he saw Jacinta. He crouched down beside her to help her stand, and his smile made her stomach jolt with relief. She was so glad he was alive.

For Jonah, all through the last few hours, while he'd bathed the sick man's wounds and administered what drugs he could, his mind had been on Jacinta. She looked tired but in none of the distress he'd feared as he'd waited to be brought to her.

His repeated questions to the chief had been met with bland assurances that she was safe in her tent as guarantee that Jonah would save the chief's son. As the night had worn on and little improvement had been seen in the patient, the chief had begun to mutter dire warnings about what would happen to the Missy-Dokkta if Jonah failed.

Thankfully, at last, in the early hours of the morning, the patient had seemed to rest more easily, and grudgingly the chief had allowed Jonah to be led to the creek to wash before returning to Jacinta.

Now, to find her drowsily awake after what he'd dreaded he would find, he was almost faint with relief.

His brain, already sluggish with physical and nervous exhaustion, totally scrambled and he struggled for something to divert how much he wanted to feel his arms around her.

Jacinta had no such qualms as she hurled herself at him and buried her nose in his chest. 'Thank God you're safe,' she said. Her arms crept around him and he felt himself sigh into her as he hugged her back.

Jonah buried his face in the top of her head and inhaled the freshness of her hair after the rankness of disease and approaching death of the last six hours, and he could feel himself smile despite their circumstances.

'They haven't hurt you?'

'No, I'm fine. You?'

'Just tired.'

'How's the patient?' she said.

His smile faded. 'Dying. It would be useful if they didn't blame us when the inevitable happens.' The words hung in the tent between them, and Jacinta swallowed the dry lump in her throat. That didn't sound promising.

Jonah put her from him and clenched his hands, and Jacinta realised this was even more dire than she'd supposed.

'Is there nothing we can do?' Jacinta needed clarification of Jonah's fears, despite a niggling fear that she'd be sorry she asked.

Jonah rested his finger across her lips as the guard poked his head into the tent and glared at them both suspiciously.

Jonah stepped in front of her and she remembered

he was no stranger to dangerous situations. There was little comfort in the thought because, no matter how skilled Jonah was, one man against a dozen couldn't win.

The guard glared at them and then flopped the tent flap back into placc. They could see the outline of his body as he planted his feet outside the flap.

Jonah glanced assessingly around the makeshift tent and then back to Jacinta's worried face.

He tipped her chin up to look at him, and he smiled as he shook his head. 'There will be no defeat in this tent. It's not over till the fat lady sings, but it's not good.'

He explained, 'Our patient is Tuma, the chief's son. His stomach wound is gangrenous and he needs more antibiotics than we have. I told the chief his son would die if he's not taken to the hospital.' He met her eyes. 'He told me if his son dies, we would die, too.'

She shook her head at the mention of death. 'What can we do?'

He shrugged. 'We continue to bathe the wound, use our antibiotics, keep the patient hydrated and hope his own immune system will eventually beat the organism. But I think that will only buy us some time—if we're lucky, a couple of days—before the inevitable happens. Septicaemia will kill him.'

The flatness of his tone removed any hope Jacinta had that they would be able to treat their way out of captivity.

Her voice felt as if it was coming from a long way

away. This all seemed surreal. 'You don't appear too perturbed about the chief's threat to kill us.'

'I'm perturbed,' he said dryly. 'The threat is real enough, but I'm not planning on us staying around long enough to let it happen. It's a good sign they haven't tied you up. When the moon sets in about an hour, we'll have a brief window of opportunity to get away.'

Her shoulders sagged with relief. Jonah seemed confident they would escape and she was glad he was experienced in this kind of situation. She suddenly thought of Mr McTash, the pilot from Port Moresby, and his experience with crash landings. You certainly gained unusual extra-curricular education here. 'So what's the plan?'

Jonah felt the weight of her expectations on his shoulders. She stood there, unintentionally leaning towards him, fragile-necked and as helpless as a new-born babe as she watched him, so sure he knew all the answers. His greatest fear stared him in the face.

Here was Melinda all over again. He felt like screaming that he didn't want this responsibility. What if he couldn't save this woman either? The thought was like a hammer blow between his shoulder blades, and he winced at the pain.

'We'll have to wait for the opportunity when it presents itself,' he said gruffly. 'They'll wake us if he takes a turn for the worse.' He paused and finished under his breath, 'Or when he dies. Maybe you should try to sleep. When we run it will be hard going in the dark.'

She tried to smile at him but her mouth wobbled at the edges. 'Thank you for saying when and not if.'

'My pleasure.'

She hesitated before she lay down. 'Will you hold me?'

Reality crashed in and he closed his eyes with the pain of loss. He couldn't let this happen to her. But she was waiting for his answer. He opened his eyes, furious with himself that she'd had to ask when her need was so great.

'May I?' he said softly, and drew her towards him. Then he stopped. 'Wait. I'll spread this blanket. It's not the softest in the world but it beats the heck out of the dirt.'

Then he lay down beside her and she snuggled into his chest with his arm behind her head and her soft cheek on his skin searing into his heart.

Her hair smelt of some citrusy shampoo and un-obtrusively he breathed in her scent more deeply. The top of her head was so close to his mouth he couldn't help the gentle kiss that he lost in the softness. That action added taste to his sensations and Jonah closed his eyes as the essence of her swirled around beneath his lids and through his body like a drug.

All the feelings he'd been suppressing since the first day he'd met her rose like a heated mist inside him. He jerked open his eyes.

It would be crazy to venture down that path, and he tipped his head back to stare at the point where the centre pole met the apex of the tarpaulin. A few stars shone through the gap in the tent and between the treetops and he couldn't believe he'd contemplated making love to her. They were in mortal danger, for Pete's sake.

Diffused light from the moon shone through the rough lashing. If it rained, the hole was big enough for them to get wet. Good. He was in need of a cold shower.

Jacinta must have noticed he'd withdrawn from her because she twisted her neck to look up at him. Her invitation or need, he wasn't sure which, made a mockery of his denial and helplessly he stared back at her, weak from his own wanting.

'Kiss me.' He wasn't sure if she said it out loud or even formed the words with her lips, but the request was there and he had no defence against that appeal. When he lowered his head, her mouth under his was so sweet and their joining so achingly tender and beautiful that he knew he would never forget it. He could do nothing else but kiss her again.

A long time later they surfaced, breathless and red-cheeked as they opened their eyes.

Jonah felt as though his heart was breaking. 'I've wanted to kiss you like that for a long time. From the first moment I saw your beautiful face.'

She smiled and doubted she'd win any pageants at the moment. But the emotion beneath his words turned them into further caresses whispered against her skin, and she smiled as she closed her eyes again so she could forget where she was and just be in his arms.

Finally she accepted the strange ache she'd had

since Jonah Armstrong had been wheeled into her world and the futility of fighting against her destiny to love him.

Aware now why she'd followed him to this country, risking everything, and in the end had gambled more than she'd planned to—because of this moment, and any moments they had left. Was he her soul mate? Was he the empty part of her heart that she'd thought would never be filled?

Here in this grubby, earthen-floored tent on a steamy, menacing night in the highlands of Papua New Guinea, she knew she'd found love. Not the floating, romantic, giggly type of love but the I-need-him-to-breathe type of love that promised heartache and agony if they were given enough time.

Off balance and confused by the magnitude of her discovery, Jacinta hugged the questions to herself for a little longer, but she couldn't help squeezing his hand and praying that at least some of her feelings were returned.

She regretted the pain she would cause to Noni and her father at her choice to come to this country, but she could not regret her discovery.

She lifted her face to Jonah's and this time she took the initiative. The restraint of his lips softened as she pressed more firmly against him. He waited, almost passive under her mouth as if testing her resolve, until the first tentative touch from her tongue ignited him.

Then he shifted his weight and took control, and she was seared by his need as he crushed her to him. This time it was different, this time she found a need in him that she hadn't realised she had the power to ignite.

There was awe in that realisation that made her want to push him further, but he loosened his hold and gentled his mouth before he put her away from him.

'I wish, my love. But this is not the place. Try to sleep,' he said. 'I want you. Don't ever doubt that. I've wanted you from the first moment I saw you. I just hope that when we are safely back at Pudjip you don't regret me telling you this.'

He eased over to lean above her, planted his hands on either side of her head and seared her with a look. 'You are the most amazing woman I have ever met.' He kissed her and then slid back reluctantly and edged to sit upright against the pole. 'Sleep. I'll keep watch.'

Jacinta sighed with frustration as she lay back and pulled her forearm over her face. She'd just received her first refusal, but the way he'd refused had made her smile through her embarrassment. She didn't regret asking, only his answer. But she'd never sleep. She sat up against the pole beside him. 'I've slept. Tell me about your sister.'

'Women,' he said mockingly, but she could tell he wasn't really annoyed. 'Melinda was like an angel, naïve and full of goodness and smiles. She believed in the good in everybody, and in the end it killed her. I should never have let her come here to be with me. Once she went outside the compound at night to aid someone when I was busy, and that was enough. I never saw her alive again.' His shoulders drooped and Jacinta realised he was tired. Of course he was.

'Rest, Jonah. Put your head in my lap. If only for half an hour. I'll wake you if I need you.'

The time passed slowly for Jacinta, but it was time she used to savour her new discovery—that she loved Jonah.

Soon the moon had set and she woke him. When they were ready, he stood at the entrance to the tent and peered around the flap at the sleeping guard.

Jonah put his hand to his lips and motioned for her to follow, but before they could get two steps away the headman that had abducted them blocked their way with his spear. He kicked the sleeping guard awake.

Almost as if he'd been expecting their escape attempt, their taller and more vigilant captor gestured for them to return to the tent.

'He was waiting.' Her voice died away as the guard entered the tent and gestured for them both to back up against the pole and sit with their hands behind their backs.

Jonah tried to reason with him but the rapid dialect was hard for Jacinta to follow and she could see the man wouldn't be swayed. He stared back implacably and gestured with his spear at Jacinta until Jonah obeyed.

Their wrists were tied and then looped together either side of the wooden pole until their shoulders touched around the pole. At least that human warmth was allowed them. The guard gave a last tug at his knots and then, satisfied he'd secured the prisoners, he left.

Jonah twined his fingers through Jacinta's for reassurance but could feel the shudder of fear in her body. He swore under his breath.

'We'll figure something out. Don't worry.' His words hung in the air and Jonah mocked himself. No, don't worry, all will be well. She didn't answer and he squeezed her hand. 'Are you all right?'

Her voice wobbled but he could see she was determined to stay strong. 'Even I know being tied up in a tent by a renegade tribe in the wilds of the Highlands is not a good scenario, Jonah. But I won't fall to pieces, if that's what you're worried about.' He heard her mutter, 'I'll do that later.' And he almost smiled.

'I think you're pretty wonderful, Dr McCloud.' He squeezed her hand again. 'And you are a beautiful kisser.'

She squeezed his fingers back and suddenly things weren't quite so bad. 'And I wouldn't want to be tied to a pole with anyone else either,' she said with pretended nonchalance. 'Now I'm going to be quiet so you can bend your fierce intellect to how we're going to get out of here.'

He could tell she was near tears, and tomorrow would be a big day one way or another. Before long he could hear the change in her breathing as she drifted into an uneasy doze.

It wasn't so easy for him. They needed to get away, they needed not to be hunted down when the chief's son died and they needed to get to safety before some other tribe or natural disaster homed in on them.

He twisted the rope they had been secured with and found no slack in the knots. The guard had probably been tying pigs to poles since he could walk. Tomorrow he'd have to find some sharp stone they could sever the rope with and hope for the best. But he wouldn't sleep yet.

CHAPTER SIX

THE morning sun crept into the tent at about the same time as sounds of the stirring camp woke Jacinta. Barely a minute later, the flap of the tent opened and an old woman followed their guard in and began to untie Jacinta's bonds.

Jonah jerked awake behind her as the old woman muttered under her breath and struggled with the twine knots. Jacinta stared at the newcomer, certain she'd seen her somewhere before.

Jonah spoke to the woman in an unfamiliar dialect, and Jacinta saw her shake her head and point to Jacinta and then herself.

'Mimi and Missy-Dokkta.' And she made a cutting motion with her hands. That's all, she seemed to say.

Jacinta remembered then. 'Mimi was in the plane I came to Hagen in,' she said over her shoulder to Jonah. 'What did she say?'

'She said the chief's son's wife is having a baby and in trouble. You'd better go with her.'

Jacinta followed Mimi across to another tent on the outskirts of the camp and the cloying smell of blood and amniotic fluid hit her nostrils and warned her of what she'd see.

The young woman on the grass mound moaned softly as she pushed with the force of the contraction and a tiny baby's breech body, the size of a large man's hand, was suspended between life and death.

Heart in throat, Jacinta was thankful for Jonah's recent lessons, and as she came closer she worried just how premature this child was. One thing at a time. She settled herself and glanced around for somewhere to wash her hands. Of course there were no facilities or even a dish of water so she wiped her hands on her shirt and apologised to the hygiene god as she neared the woman.

Anchored by his head, the baby's tiny body was mottled blue as he lay suspended between intra- and extra-uterine life. Jacinta glanced at Mimi and pointed to herself and the baby, seeking permission.

'Yes. Quick-quick.' The old woman nodded with some urgency and Jacinta drew a deep breath. So much for 'hands-off breech'.

Jacinta tried to smile at the half-conscious woman as she lay her down in reassurance and knelt down on the dirt. Then she realised why this baby looked different. The belly was facing upwards and the baby's head was already chin up and could not extend further to be born.

When she checked the crease in the little one's neck for a hidden umbilical cord, sure enough, the slowly pulsating rope was looped around the baby's neck as well.

'Rotate the baby from face up to face down,' she muttered to herself, 'and slip the cord over the head if you can.'

The tightness of the cord around his neck made it

impossible for Jacinta to do much other than cut the lifeline prior to birth. The idea was unattractive without a clamp or even a piece of string to stop foetal haemorrhage.

'String? I need string or twine to tie the cord and a knife.' She mimed the tying off of the cord to Mimi and cutting motions.

Mimi asked around the gathered women and one of them produced a wicked-looking knife, which she handed to Jacinta. For the string Mimi just shrugged that she didn't understand.

Jacinta felt like screaming until she calmed herself with a deep breath. OK. Think laterally.

She gestured for Mimi to come over and grasp the umbilical cord a few inches from the baby's belly and squeeze very hard. If the maternal end of the cord bled it would not be catastrophic, but if blood drained from this tiny baby, things would quickly deteriorate. She'd think of a cord tie in a minute.

Quickly Jacinta cut the cord and unwound the now free end from the baby's neck. As soon as the anchor was gone, she rotated the baby slowly to face down and the little boy slid out into Jacinta's hands and lay flaccidly like a stunned fish, with his dark eyes staring unblinkingly up at her.

At least the baby's end of the cord was long, she consoled herself as she tied one knot in the slippery rope and then another one.

'That's what I call a true knot,' she muttered to herself and concentrated on his resuscitation.

Jacinta pulled the blanket over him, rubbing his

body quickly through the material to stimulate him to breathe as well as dry him. His feeble cry was greeted by a sudden babble of voices and even the new mother opened her eyes and smiled before she lapsed back into her stupor.

Don't celebrate too early, Jacinta thought grimly, because she'd bet the infant was at least six weeks early and would be touch and go in such primitive conditions.

A sudden gush of blood heralded the next complication and she concentrated on the mother as the placenta was delivered. The baby could nestle between his mother's breasts while Jacinta worried about the flood of bright blood that had begun at the bottom of the makeshift bed.

Basics, she urged herself, and firmly massaged the woman's uterus through the recently stretched abdominal wall until the red torrent slowed and finally stopped. Jacinta quickly dabbed away the blood to check for tissue trauma before the next gush began. She couldn't see anything that would cause bleeding so that left the muscular contraction of the uterus as the most likely candidate.

'Rub here.' She mimed how Mimi should find the top of the new mother's uterus and massage her abdomen to help start the contraction of the uterus and constriction of the source of bleeding.

Mimi nodded and calmly continued that job while Jacinta wiped her hands on the edge of the blanket and leaned up to peer under the blanket at the new baby. His tiny face screwed up under the thick coating of white vernix that almost glued his eyes shut, but despite his size he looked perfect.

When he let out a mewing cry Jacinta gestured to his mother's breast and mimed squeezing colostrum into the baby's mouth. If the newborn was to have any chance, he needed warmth and ideally at least a couple of mils of expressed colostrum dripped into his mouth every hour.

As she sat back on her hands her eyes fell on the bloodstained knife that rested beside her foot, unnoticed by the women who were distracted as they cooed over the new baby.

Unobtrusively she glanced around and leaned towards the new mother. Her right hand fell down beside her leg until she found the knife. With her dominant hand Jacinta gently rubbed the mother's stomach again and curled the fingers of the other around the wooden handle. She nudged the implement slowly until it was cold and sticky inside her sock.

No doubt Mimi's friend would miss her knife, but hopefully she wouldn't connect its disappearance with Jacinta.

The baby was being cared for and there was nothing else she could do there. Jacinta avoided Mimi's eyes as she shifted position and couldn't wait to see Jonah with her prize. Her knees protested as she eased out of her cramped stance and arched her back to dissipate the tension from it. As she looked around the circle of faces, she noticed a small girl watching her with wary eyes. Instinctively she smiled as if she hadn't just broken their trust and stolen from them.

The girl glanced down at Jacinta's ankle and then away, and the cold hand of dread settled in her stomach. It had been worth a try, she consoled herself as she waited for the outbreak of recriminations. Instead, she was congratulated by the women and Mimi pointed to the young mother and introduced her. 'Neena.'

'Congratulations, Neena,' Jacinta said to the new mother, and then she was ushered out.

She was escorted back towards their tent and nothing had been said about the knife. Jacinta motioned towards the nearby creek and mimed washing her hands. Mimi gestured assent and followed Jacinta to the water's edge.

Crystal clear and icy cold, the water swirled away the drying blood from her fingers, and she sighed with pleasure as she dug her fingers into the sandy bottom to loosen any blood under her fingernails. She splashed her face but before she could get carried away with her ablutions Mimi poked her in the back and hurried her not unkindly back up the incline towards the tent.

At least she hadn't tied her up again, Jacinta thought as she was left alone in the tent once more. Jonah must have been recalled to duty on the chief's son. That was the only scenario her brain would allow her to contemplate, and she glanced around for a place to hide the knife in case they came back to search her.

With an effort she managed to make a thin shaft in the soil beside the wooden base of the central pole, and pushed the knife into it until the handle top was level with the surface. She dusted dirt over the top but not deeply, so that if their hands were tied again that night, hopefully Jonah would be able to retrieve it.

No sooner had she brushed her hands as free of dirt as she could than Mimi returned with a guard, and the suspicion in her eyes was clear. She gestured for Jacinta to turn around and searched her thoroughly. The bloodstained sock caused no comment as there were other stains elsewhere on her clothing. Satisfied, though unhappily, that Jacinta didn't have the knife, Mimi left.

When Jonah was pushed inside the tent a few minutes later Jacinta didn't wait for an invitation as she launched herself at him. When his arms closed around her she sagged with relief and buried her head in his chest.

'I'm pleased to see you, too. What's this in aid of?' his voice rumbled from above her ear, and she breathed in the unmistakable male scent of him, comforted by the fact that he was solidly around her. She could feel the palpitations in her own chest, and the regular thump of Jonah's heart was infinitely reassuring. They were safe for the time being.

His finger slid under her chin and he tilted her face so he could see her expression. 'Are you OK?' Concern slashed his brow as he began to suspect she wasn't.

'I'm fine now.' She pulled out of his arms reluctantly and stepped back, trying hard to maintain a smile. 'It was a big morning. I had some news and you weren't here.' She chewed her lip ruefully. 'And when you didn't come back, I started to worry. And then they searched me for the knife and it was pretty scary.'

'What knife?' he said.

Typical male, Jacinta thought. Go straight to what interests you. But she was proud of her ingenuity. 'The knife I stole and buried beside the pole so we can cut our ropes tonight.'

A slow smile spread across his face and he tugged her back into his arms for a brief hug and then held her away from him to look into her face. She couldn't tell what he was thinking but there was warmth in his blue eyes.

'You continue to surprise me.' His voice dropped as he lowered his head, and then his lips touched hers and he closed his eyes as he savoured the taste of her. The kiss was gentle, but conveyed myriad messages that confirmed he cared before he let her go. 'So many pleasant surprises,' he mused. 'Where did you get the knife?'

She told him of the birth and his enthusiastic approval did nothing to settle the tumult his kiss had stirred.

'How is the chief's son?' she asked for distraction, and watched his eyes darken with concern.

'Tuma has rallied a little but I think his improvement is that false hope you sometimes see before a patient fades.'

Jacinta nodded. She'd seen it many times, too. Critical patients seemed to wake and respond for a brief time before lapsing back into unconsciousness, never to wake again.

'How much time do you think we have?'

Jonah met her look squarely, aware she deserved the truth but reluctant to worry her unnecessarily. 'To-night—tomorrow at the latest. But it's a catch twenty-two situation. If we escape, our trail has to be a couple of hours old for them not to risk following us, so we need to pick our moment to run.'

CHAPTER SEVEN

SEVERAL hours after dark, when the night birds began their raucous cries for food, there was a commotion in the camp. A sudden lone female wailed loudly in grief and then the mournful sound swelled as more voices acknowledged someone's passing.

Jonah met Jacinta's eyes as he moved over to the entrance to listen to the guards' conversation. He nodded as if he'd already known. 'Tuma is dead.'

He watched Jacinta as his words sank in and instinctively he moved back to support her.

She moistened her lips and formed the words he'd been dreading.

'When…when will they come for us?'

He hated to see the look of trepidation in her eyes but he knew the same must be reflected in his own face.

'Soon.' There was no time to plan any kind of resistance or flight. The entrance flap to the tent was yanked back and a tribesman gestured for them both to follow him. This time the point of his spear was less reticent about hurting them and pricked their backs as they were nudged none too gently towards the chief's hut.

It was eerie, crossing the camp. Campfires burned in several places, and the women and children huddled together as they keened outside their tents. Stone-faced tribesmen stared implacably at the white doctors who had failed their chief and his son, and there was no comfort to be had on the trek to hear their fate.

The chief's head was bowed when they entered the tent and Jacinta could smell the infection that had killed Tuma. The young man's body lay still and silent.

The chief launched into a tirade against Jonah, who stared back expressionless until the old man finished. Jacinta struggled to pick up a few of the rapidly spoken words and those she recognised struck fear into her heart.

Jonah's expression didn't change and Jacinta prayed she'd misinterpreted. If anything, the chief's grief increased as Jonah chose his words. His tone was quiet and even, as if dealing with a fractious patient. He paused and drew Jacinta next to him, until she stood firm against his side, united with Jonah against the old man.

The chief shrugged, spat and grunted, and then turned away from them. The guard that had accompanied them gestured for them to leave.

'Tell me,' Jacinta whispered as they were prodded back to their tent.

'The chief says we die when the sun rises tomorrow.'

The words were no less horrific for the quiet way they were spoken, but something didn't make sense. 'I heard him say ''now''.'

Jonah smiled grimly. 'He did, but I suggested we at least deserved another night alive together.'

There was something about the way he said 'together' that seemed to hold a key to the chief changing his mind, and she mulled over it as they crossed the now deserted camp.

Jonah admired that her back remained unbowed as she walked and he ached with how much she'd come to mean to him. She was worthy of a better man than he, but she wouldn't have that chance now.

No sign of hysterics, though probably it was her misguided blind faith that he'd still find a way out of this mess. His fists clenched with frustration. He was all out of ideas at the moment. Even now, they had been so close to immediate death that he couldn't believe they had a stay of execution.

He needed to gather his reserves for the next fight. His heart ached with regret because he knew there was little he could do now that the chief had decreed their death. The old man would be doubly suspicious that they would try to escape.

Jacinta ducked inside the tent in front of him. 'We have to escape.'

Jonah saw her glance around the tent for inspiration and he wished he could comfort her. She was so full of life and had so much to offer, both as a doctor and a woman, let alone the anguish of knowing she would never see her family again. He should have left her at the hospital where at least she had the compound to keep her safe.

If there was some way he could get her to safety,

it didn't matter if he didn't make it. No one was waiting for him at home.

He'd tried. That first day he'd asked the chief to let her go and he would gladly stay, but the old man had had none of it.

Tonight he'd offered everything he could imagine to sway the chief from killing Jacinta. Money and medicinal drugs—which he'd never have believed he'd even pretend to promise. But the old man had been adamant they should pay for Tuma's death.

Jacinta clenched her hands. 'So that's it? We just sit here and wait for them to come and kill us in the morning? It seems so bizarre. So pointless. Is there nothing we can do in the meantime?'

He shrugged. 'We can fight now, but before you could run they would cut us both down, and I'd rather not have their blood on my hands for no reason. Even if they leave us untied, it will be difficult as they've put more guards outside the tent. Maybe the men will sleep in the early hours of the morning so that we can slip away, but it will be much harder now that Tuma is dead.'

'Why would they leave us untied when they tied us last night?'

'Does it matter?' He didn't meet her eyes. Maybe he should tell her it was because the chief had agreed he could make her his wife before the morning. Jonah didn't know why he'd suggested it to the old man, but the request had at least worked temporarily. It had helped when he'd reminded the chief of Jacinta's part in saving his grandson.

'Our only chance is to sneak away when the camp is asleep.' He didn't say it but at the moment he could see very little hope of that. No guard would risk a newly bereaved chief's wrath by sleeping and allowing the prisoners to escape—especially having been caught the previous night.

He needed to regather his mental energy, battle this inertia that was seeping into him. He hadn't slept at all last night, terrified that some of the men would come and take Jacinta for sport, but it hadn't happened. He needed clarity of mind to plan their escape if he could just forget the danger to Jacinta for a while.

'We have time to pass before we can even think about doing anything. They will leave us alone for the time being.'

She looked up suspiciously. 'How do you know that?'

'Why do you have to ask questions when I'm asking questions?' He pretended to frown.

She wasn't fooled. 'There's something suspicious about a death sentence and no bonds and something not genuine about a twelve-hour reprieve. And there's something you are not telling me.'

He looked into her eyes then and a gentle smile hovered where no smile should have been. 'True.' He watched her take in his admission and she turned away before he could read what conclusion she'd drawn. That was the problem—she was far from slow-witted.

'What are you not telling me?'

She wouldn't give up, but then, he'd known she wouldn't. 'That you are tenacious and annoying and brilliant and a great doctor, and you scare the living daylights out of me.' She may as well know the lot.

The rest he said slowly. 'The last person I loved died in this country, too, and I can't bear the thought of not being able to save you either. I told the chief that he owed it to us to give us one more night together, and he agreed.'

She blinked back the tears that his words triggered, and bit her lip.

He brushed her cheek with his finger. 'Is there any chance of one of those kisses we had last night? I'm sorely in need of a little comfort and you are so very good at making me feel better.'

Jacinta blinked and, despite his banter, she could hear the need in his words. He needed her! The concept was harder to comprehend than pidgin English. Did Jonah mean he cared for her? At the very least it was proof her feelings weren't one-sided, and through all the fear and uncertainty today, at the back of her mind the memory of last night's closeness had sustained her.

Then his previous words sank in. The last time he'd loved someone—that meant he loved someone now. Her?

He opened his arms. 'Come here and kiss me.' It was almost an order.

In another time and place she might have wanted to continue the argument, explore the beginnings of wonder that they loved each other. Maybe banter with him and pit her wits against his. But the time wasn't right. Every moment was precious now and she stepped into his embrace with a sigh of relief. His hand brushed the hair from her forehead as he looked deep into her eyes, and she absorbed the sight of his dear face like dry earth absorbing rain.

'In another time and place I won't always come so placidly, you know,' she whispered as he came closer.

'I'll look forward to it,' he said, and his mouth brushed hers. There was no further inclination for talking as their needs rose in a swell of emotion that lifted them both away from their circumstances and transported them to a much sweeter place.

But they couldn't stay there for ever. A shout from outside the tent reminded them of their danger and they stepped apart. A guard pulled back a quarter of the flap and slid a drooping leaf with fruit and a mug of water onto the floor beside the entrance.

Jacinta stared fearfully at the man but he didn't meet her eyes as he backed out. She buried her face in Jonah's chest again as her heart rate settled and she accepted that the tribesmen hadn't changed their minds about the time to kill them yet. 'We've wasted so much time and there's so little left,' she said.

'We should eat because we'll need our strength.'

'Why would they feed us when they want to kill us?'

He crouched down beside the offering and began to divide the fruit. 'They are being polite.'

Jacinta shook her head. 'Can't they be rude and not kill us?'

'Good plan.'

Jacinta sighed. 'You've changed again and I don't understand you.'

'We still have the rest of the night to get away, we have to focus on that. We have your knife, we have each other and we have several hours to wait, and then we escape before it starts getting light. But I'm so tired I can hardly see straight.'

She saw it then. The burden he carried, the fear that was mostly for her and the strain as he racked his brain for a solution to their dilemma. She could share some of his responsibilities, if only for a short while. She moved over to crouch beside him. 'We'll eat, and we'll lie down together and then you sleep for a little while and I'll keep watch.'

'Doctor's orders, Jacinta?' The weariness was there behind his smile and she knew he couldn't refuse.

'Absolutely. Rest, Jonah.' They drew comfort from each other as they ate their fruit and slaked their thirst. When they were finished, Jonah pushed the remains outside the tent to prevent the risk of any stray animals searching the tent to forage. She gathered their things as if ready for flight. If they escaped, the medicines they had were too precious to leave.

Half an hour later, with his head in her lap, Jonah breathed deeply in sleep, and the harsh lines in his face relaxed as he entrusted their safety to her. Jacinta sat upright against the pole and listened to the sound of the camp settling around them, and every few minutes the guards outside their tent grunted to each other.

Jacinta's mind roved over the last few weeks and the strange emotions she'd felt at each new experience. She had such huge admiration for the hospital staff and the missionaries, and felt horror at the brutality she'd seen, the beauty of the tropical night and the simplicity and innocence of the children. Everything seemed so much larger than life here.

But nothing was larger in her life than Jonah. She wondered at the boy he must have been before he'd turned into the responsible man he'd become. Was there a time he'd been carefree or had he always been bowed with the misfortunes of others and his role in their care? What had his parents been like, and exactly what had happened to his sister?

He ran the hospital not like the dictator she'd first thought, although he certainly expected to be obeyed, but like an older brother. He kept his finger on the pulse not just of his patients but all his staff and their families, too. As he slept, she memorised his face. He needed to delegate more, realise that others could carry the load he shouldered too often on his own.

Like he shouldered the responsibility of getting them out of there, but there was no reason she couldn't think up just as good an escape plan as he could.

Jacinta glanced around the dark tent again, straining for inspiration. She sighed and her eyes fell on the medicine tote she'd packed in preparation for their escape. Maybe there was something she could find in there to help.

Perhaps if she listed their assets, an idea would come to her. She had nothing else to do.

Their main asset was Jonah. He was experienced, brave, knew the area and the enemy, and hopefully when he woke he would be refreshed enough to sort out any details of the great plan she would come up with.

Their second asset was the knife—something their captors didn't know they had.

Their third was the medicine kit. It was a possible resource she hadn't given a lot of thought to, but she could remedy that shortsightedness now.

Jacinta stretched her arm carefully across and grasped the handle of the rucksack, anxious not to disturb Jonah's sleep as he lay with his head in her lap. He stirred with her sideways movement and his eyelids flickered with the slight dragging noise the bag made as it bumped across towards her. Instinctively she stroked his brow and he sighed and settled back into slumber without opening his eyes.

Quietly, when the bag rested against her hip, she began to pull out the contents one by one and place them on the dirt floor beside her, just making out the objects in the dark.

Their water-purifying and antimalarial tablets and the vial of salt for leeches lay on top. Then the tourniquet, cannulas and intravenous tubing to run a drip, a bag of saline, some sticking plaster, dressings and two bandages. The tiny blood-pressure cuff and stethoscope had potential as they were made up of several components, some of which surely could be useful.

She rummaged at the bottom of the bag and found a penlight she'd forgotten about and the zippered compartment of drug ampoules and tablets.

The only anaesthetic drugs they had were short-acting muscle relaxants and she mulled over the logistics of administering a drug to someone without them becoming aware of the fact. Fancifully she saw herself injecting a guard with an anaesthetic through the lining of the tent. Perhaps he'd brush the sting away like a mosquito. Perhaps he'd run her through with his spear. She really was better equipped to deal with the concrete jungle of Sydney.

She rummaged through the last of the drugs. There were antihypertensives, Adrenalin for shock, Valium for fits and two ampoules Morphine for pain. All in all a slim selection but not without some use.

Apart from the logistics of administration, if they could render the guards unconscious, they could slit the back of the tent and escape into the night. Her mind twisted and darted through scenarios of escape, and the time passed.

When Jonah woke up the hut was dark, but without looking at her he knew Jacinta's features as if it were midday in the sun. She would be frowning, with those black brows of hers drawn as she concentrated. Unless a miracle arrived—or the cavalry—he believed they would die in a few hours. He just hoped it would be swiftly. Especially for Jacinta.

'Come down here, Jacinta.' She looked down at his

open eyes and smiled. His tone was softer than she'd ever heard it and it was too dark to read his face. She snuggled down beside him and rested her head on his arm, which he had tucked under her.

He didn't know where to start but how tragic it would be if he left what was in his heart until it was too late. 'Our escape hasn't gone to plan and there's a chance we may not make it home,' he said. 'There are things that should be said between us should anything happen.'

Jacinta was jerked right out of her heroic daydreams. 'What happened to waiting for the fat lady to sing? What happened to never give up?'

'Of course we won't give up, and I'll protect you with my life. If an opportunity arises, we take it, but this is about us and about something that can't be changed, no matter what happens in the morning.'

He took her face in his hands and in the darkness the whites of his eyes burned into hers. He drew a deep breath and spoke the words he'd never dreamt of saying. 'I love you. I've never said that to another woman in my entire life. I love your strengths and your weaknesses and your beauty and your feistiness.' He shrugged and smiled as he hugged her. 'I love all of you.'

She didn't know what to say. It was too tragic and amazing and she couldn't quite believe him because it all sounded too pat. 'This is great timing, Jonah. We die in a few hours and now you love me. I would have liked a few more hours to enjoy this.'

'Stop it, Jacinta. I want to make love to you but I

want it to be right. I don't want to take advantage of
you or cheapen something so beautiful. I want you to
marry me. Here, in the dark of this hut, just the two
of us before God, because I have finally found you.'

His voice trailed away and she realised he was serious and how hard it must have been for him to even
consider they wouldn't make it. She'd known he had
courage but she didn't think she had the strength to
think past that night. Now she had to.

He found her hand in the dark and stroked the inside of her palm. 'You know I love you! Don't you?
I never thought I would love as I love you and, despite the irony and circumstances of our time together,
the finding of such a love should be celebrated. I owe
it to you and to myself because we should honour
something so strong. For however long we live. Will
you become my wife tonight?'

Imprisoned together, and sure of death, Jonah's
proposal blurred her eyes with tears. Just the two of
them, in a marriage she'd never dreamt of, unpreten-
tious yet full of symbolism for only them.

She loved Jonah, had realised that earlier and de-
spaired of how that love would cope in their everyday
lives. But this wasn't everyday. This was a tent in an
enemy camp and they would probably die in a few
hours. She could die Jacinta McCloud or Jacinta
Armstrong—avowed wife of the one man she'd ever
loved and who loved her.

At least they would die together. She looked up at
him and there was no denying they had a bond.

'I don't know if our marriage would work in the

real world, but I do love you with all my heart and I would be honoured to marry you.'

He took both her hands in his and they knelt down facing each other beside the centre pole. A few stars could be seen if they looked through the gap in the roof.

The first bird of the early morning woke and began calling to its mate, and although dawn hadn't broken there was less darkness in the night.

Jonah's voice came out of the dimness, quietly but full of strength and sureness, and the shiver of goose-flesh ran down her arms at the poignancy. 'I, Jonah Gage Armstrong, here in this tent in the wilds of the New Guinea mountains, take you, Jacinta McCloud, to be my wife. To have and to hold, through richer and poorer, through sickness and in health, from this day forward, till death us do part.'

When she followed his lead and repeated the words without stumbling, he watched her steadily and his hands tightened over hers as she completed the vow.

He tugged off his sister's signet ring from his little finger and took her hand to single out her ring finger.

'Will you wear my ring until I can buy you a proper one?' They both knew there was little chance of that happening, but it made the moment even more poignant. He slid the finely wrought ring onto her finger over her knuckle, and it rested as if sized exactly for that place on her hand.

They both stared at the symbol between them. 'I would be honoured,' she whispered.

'May I kiss the bride?' he asked teasingly.

'She'd be very disappointed if you didn't.'

'Welcome, Mrs Armstrong,' he whispered as his lips lowered to hers. She breathed the word 'husband' as she met him, determined not to shy from the hugeness of the moment. She'd dreamt of this. She wanted it. She just hoped he didn't mind her inexperience.

He must have seen her determination because he shook his head in admiration. 'Are you afraid of *anything*?'

'Only of not satisfying you.' Then she tilted her chin to be honest. 'I'm no hero. I'm terrified of dying, of the morning, but we have this moment.' She lifted her hands up to circle his neck and his face came closer. 'I think I've found a way to keep the fear away.'

They kissed and then naturally, slowly he unbuttoned her blouse, and the cool night air brushed her skin. Her arms goosefleshed again, though whether from the coolness or the heat of his look she wasn't sure, but the feeling was one she savoured. He continued and slid her free of all restraints and then his own before he lay beside her on their clothes.

He rose on one elbow and with the other hand he traced the outlines of her body. Then his mouth followed where his fingers had led until she was trembling with need. Every time she lifted her hand to touch him he settled it back by her side again and urged her to leave him to his work.

She tossed her head with the multitude of sensations and bit her lip to keep silent. Finally he slowed and his lips returned to her face. With one searing kiss his face lifted away from her as he rose above her, and when he slowly entered her they stared into each other's eyes in the gloom until their lips met again.

Slowly he rocked and she held her breath in tiny gasps until he drove deeper and she rose to meet him. His chest was rock solid against hers and the taste of his skin on her tongue would be something she would never forget. That, and belonging, even briefly, to Jonah.

This moment was divinely right and she gloried in the force between them and in the surging joy that rose inside her. Her body thrummed and he moaned her name in a deep whisper that teetered her on the edge until together they seemed to rise into the sky in a myriad of lights that left her shaking. Finally her breathing slowed and she lay against him, exhausted yet more alive than she had ever been. He hugged her to him and she dozed with his strong arms around her.

Later, they joined once more and he stifled her cries of joy with his mouth. Softly murmuring their dreams and their secrets, they came to know each other intimately and made poignant love until the dawn began to break properly. They even whispered of the chance that for one night they could have created life between them before they died.

They dressed and all that was left was to wait for the tribesmen to come for them.

The flap pulled back and, instead of the fierce

guards, Mimi burst in and gestured for Jacinta to follow her.

Jacinta heard Jonah ask questions and the old
woman threw her answers over her shoulder as she
hurried out, dragging Jacinta by the arm behind her.
Jacinta looked back once and saw the guard pushing
Jonah back inside the tent with his spear. Her heart
raced with the suddenness of her summons as she
hurried after the old woman.

They returned to the tent she'd been in the previous
morning. Her fears for the health of the baby seemed
unfounded. The tiny mite was bundled against another
woman and was sucking vigorously at his milk-
mother's breast.

It was the newly widowed mother who needed her
assistance. Neena jerked uncontrollably on the earth
floor and her eyes rolled in her head as she was
thrown about with the force of the convulsions. The
mound of covers shook as she jerked with the fit, and
her pink lips had turned blue with the lack of respi-
ratory effort. She needed drugs and they were back
in the tent. Jacinta turned to Mimi and sketched her
rucksack with her hands.

'Dokkta bag. Hurry,' she said, and the meaning of
her command was clear even though their languages
weren't compatible. Mimi rushed off and Jacinta
called after her for Jonah's help but held little hope
that the she would bring him, too.

Jacinta knelt beside the young woman and tipped
her firmly on her side into the recovery position, unable to stop the prolonged fit without medication.

It now seemed likely the reason Neena had gone into labour early had been pre-eclampsia. In the last few hours the woman's thin face had become round with fluid and it was likely her blood pressure was extremely high. The damage to her kidneys Jacinta didn't want to think about.

Mimi returned and thrust the rucksack at Jacinta, who took it, unsurprised that Jonah hadn't been allowed to come.

Neena's convulsions slowly stilled and her gasping breath signalled the end of one fit and a respite for everyone watching.

Eager to cannulate her before the next fit, Jacinta asked Mimi to hold Neena's hand while she inserted the intravenous line before the next fit made the procedure more difficult.

She injected the antihypertensive and anticonvulsant and over the next half-hour they watched anxiously as the young woman's cerebral irritation decreased.

An hour later the young woman seemed to be sleeping peacefully and Jacinta left two strips of blood pressure tablets with Mimi to be issued three times a day until they ran out. It was all she could do.

Mimi tapped Jacinta on the arm and thanked her as she drew her away from the resting woman.

When they left the tent, they didn't head back across the camp but away towards the creek, and Jacinta assumed she was being allowed to wash again. She put down the bag and sluiced her arms.

The old woman seemed furtive in her movements and glanced repeatedly over her shoulder to ensure no one was watching them.

'We go now, follow creek, cross bridge, head to road, then I come back.'

Jacinta stared, open-mouthed. 'My friend. The other doctor. I can't leave without him.'

'Him dead. When I get bag long time ago. He fight, they kill him. Dead.'

'Not true.' Jacinta looked back up to the camp and she saw group of men around a fallen figure. Cold fear brought the nausea to her throat. 'You're tricking me.'

'No' She shook her wizened face sadly. 'Saw him go down with bad head. You bin good, you not die. Already took his clothes and boots. We go now, I come back quick-quick.'

Jacinta felt as though the woman was talking through a long tunnel and she could barely hear her. All she could hear were the words 'Him dead.'

She tried to search in her mind for that sureness she'd had earlier that Jonah was alive, but now, when she needed it most, that reassurance eluded her.

Mimi darted off into the jungle alongside the creek and Jacinta stared after her in a grieving daze as she picked up the doctor's bag.

'Quick-quick,' the old woman whispered.

The hours blurred for Jacinta as Mimi hurried her along barely discernible tracks at breakneck speed. She should be grateful but all she could think of was Jonah and the chance that Mimi was mistaken.

Branches slapped her cheeks viciously, roots tangled around her feet as the tears rolled down her face, and time seemed to run into itself so that she didn't know if minutes or hours had passed. All through the mad rush of the day she hung onto the bag as though she wasn't letting Jonah down by carrying it.

Finally Mimi stopped and pointed ahead. 'Road there. Walk for moon.' Then she was gone.

Jacinta stood on the edge of the jungle and the only sounds were the harsh stridor of her own breath and the crack of the undergrowth from scurrying animals and birds.

She stumbled out onto the beaten earth of the road, and all she wanted to do was lie down on the dirt and curl herself into a ball where she could go to sleep and wake up with all of this a bad dream.

Her shadow stretched behind her when she turned back towards the spot she'd left the jungle. She'd never find the way back, and Jonah had told her if she had the chance to run then he would have more chance without her. But what if he wasn't dead? What if he was hurt and unable to escape because of his injuries? What if she'd gone back and been able to do something to help him escape?

She faced the sinking crescent moon above her and began to plod woodenly onward. She had little choice now but she would never forgive herself for leaving.

CHAPTER EIGHT

WHEN Jonah woke up, he was naked and against a tree. An old woman was watching and he wondered if she was responsible for him still breathing or responsible for his lack of clothes. The pain in his head rose and fell in waves with his breathing like a swaying branding-iron behind his eyes.

He had no idea how long he'd been unconscious, or why he wasn't at Pudjip, and it hurt too much to try and remember.

The trek to Pudjip was long and arduous and he fell many times. Without the old woman he would have faltered long ago. When they finally came to the compound, the cries of the gatekeeper were a welcome sound but Jonah didn't stay conscious long enough to enjoy it.

When he next began to take in his surroundings it was to the familiar routine sounds of the hospital, and Jonah realised the events of the last few days remained elusive.

Below the fog in his mind a panicked urgency fluttered to get out, and his heart pounded with the need to remember. Sometimes a whisper of an elusive feminine voice from his past clamoured for his attention.

Always it said the same thing. 'Jonah? Can you hear me?' There was something about her voice that calmed him. The nightmare receded as he clawed his way up through the mists of confusion.

He remembered saying, 'Melinda's ring.' And then the man in the next bed cried out and Jonah opened his eyes. There was no woman or voice, just the long hospital ward of Pudjip.

Some instinct made him swing his legs out the side of the bed to render his fellow patient assistance, but before his feet could touch the floor Carla hurried towards him.

'Back in your bed, Dr Armstrong, please. Dr Ford be here soon. You stay resting till doctor comes.'

When she saw that Jonah was in no more danger of standing, she hurried to the other man and soothed his distress. To Jonah's relief, Chuck Ford appeared at his side and after a moment's hesitation he perched awkwardly on Jonah's bed.

'It's good to see you alive, Jonah.'

'And you, Chuck. What happened to me? Why was I out in the jungle?'

'You were kidnapped by tribesmen four days ago on your way to the Sepik.' Chuck's explanation was careful and Jonah had the impression he was trying not to upset him. 'What can you remember?'

Jonah closed his eyes and tried to remember the events of the last few days. But remember what? 'Today is Thursday?' He looked up for confirmation, and Chuck nodded.

'I had a one in seven chance of that being right, so I'm not cheering yet.'

'Try the date,' Chuck urged gently.

Jonah stared down at the sheet for a moment and then looked up. 'I can remember Christmas. So is it late December?'

Chuck didn't meet Jonah's eyes but he nodded as if he'd confirmed something he'd suspected. 'Today is the fourth of March.'

Jonah forced down the panic to remember something incredibly important, and his voice was even. 'How long did you say I was missing?'

'Four days.'

'So you're saying I have a three-month amnesia from something that happened in those four days?'

'There is no doubt you sustained some major blow to the head. The X-rays we took show a hairline fracture to the skull. It shouldn't cause you any further trouble but, of course, any small aircraft flying is out for a few weeks.'

Jonah's knuckles whitened on the bed. He needed to remember. 'Was anyone with me when I was kidnapped?'

'There was a volunteer doctor, Jacinta McCloud, from Sydney, but she's returned to Australia. Jacinta was told you'd been killed. The poor girl was distraught.' Chuck's voice was carefully expressionless.

'Was she injured? How did she get away?'

'She's fine. Some old woman she'd helped took her to the road and thankfully she was picked up by a plantation owner.'

Jonah sat up straighter. 'There was an old woman with me. She said she found me in the jungle but didn't know why I was there. Where is she?'

'We saw no one else. The gatekeeper said you stumbled out of the jungle on your own.'

Jonah sank his head in his hands. The name Jacinta McCloud struck no chord of recognition and the old woman would be long gone. At least the amnesia was focal and he remembered who and where he was. It was the 'when' that eluded him. He'd just have to wait for his memory to come back.

The next week saw Jonah quickly regain his strength, although he had to relearn the details of the patients that were missing from his memory. They thought it a great joke that the doctor could not remember them. To make matters worse, Chuck was soon due to complete his term at Pudjip and they would be short-handed for medicos again before the next volunteers arrived.

Pressed for time and manpower, Jonah worried less about his lost memories, and when the panic came in the form of dreams and fractured scenes in the middle of the night, he fought to shake off the memories and concentrate on the day ahead. But the feeling of emotional bleakness stayed with him.

From the time the Jeep from a coffee plantation picked Jacinta up, all through the inquisition by the Papuan police, and even the overwhelming grief at the Pudjip hospital, reality passed in a blur. She remembered little of the flight back to Sydney arranged by her father's consulate friend or being bundled into a car by her father and taken home to Burra.

Her first clear memory was being held by Noni and

reassured she was safe as she was tucked into bed. Her heart wept for Jonah and half the time she wished she'd never followed Mimi from the camp, but a tiny part of her couldn't help but savour the crackle of fresh sheets against her skin. She couldn't help be glad to have survived to be home again—but guilt weighed her down that she hadn't gone back to die with Jonah.

She told no one of their secret marriage because she didn't want to desecrate the memory with other people's curiosity. She tried to imagine Jonah here in Burra or even her own home if he'd lived, working with her at Pickford's day in and day out, eating at smart restaurants, knowing they needed him at Pudjip and trapped in a life he didn't want. The picture didn't fit but neither did it heal the grief and guilt.

Gradually, over the next few weeks, after she returned to her own home in Sydney, Jacinta came to the realisation that Jonah had died doing what he wanted—risking all and accepting the dangers in that harsh land because of his ideals.

A few weeks more and she was even able to feel privileged that she had been able to share such precious times with him, but the space in her heart where he lived still bled with the pain of her loss and she couldn't see the agony ever receding.

Seven weeks after her return to Australia, she woke to swirling nausea and a clarity of mind that left her stunned.

She hugged her stomach. Jonah's child. If anyone

had told her that she would risk having a baby again, she would have called them a fool.

But she was glad. Fiercely so. This was one thing she could do for Jonah. This way he would never leave her. She could raise their child with the knowledge of his or her father and in a loving home. Goodness knew what her own father would say, but they would be a family.

She hugged her stomach again and her throat ached for what might have been. She refused to contemplate that her growing baby would suffer the same congenital heart problems as Olivia. She was sure her baby would be fine.

Time dragged and she decided to return to work at Pickford's until she had to leave. Her time at Pudjip had certainly rounded out her experience as an emergency doctor.

On her first day back, Jacinta was hailed by a distraught taxi driver at the ambulance entrance.

The thin, nervous-looking man alternated between wringing his hands and gesturing wildly. 'She's having a baby in my taxi.'

Jacinta stifled a smile at the man's distress, not sure if the cabbie was more worried about his passenger or the possible mess in his vehicle.

When she arrived with nurse and wheelchair in tow, Jacinta forgot the man as she concentrated on the young woman in the rear seat of the car.

Jacinta slid along the seat next to her. 'Hi there,

I'm Jacinta, a doctor. Let me help you. Can you tell me your name?'

The young woman turned huge frightened eyes towards Jacinta, whimpered once and then drew a shaky breath to calm herself.

'Stephanie Mills. I think the baby is coming, Doctor.'

'OK.' Jacinta patted Stephanie's arm. 'You're doing fine. Tell me what you are feeling now.'

Stephanie drew another shuddering breath and swallowed. 'I think there is something hanging out down there and I don't know whether to push or what.'

A few months ago that observation would have given Jacinta heart failure while she waited for the obstetric team to arrive, but after her time in Pudjip she had a little more faith in nature. 'Well, hopefully it's a baby rather than the umbilical cord, but I need to have a quick look.' She met the girl's eyes and smiled, and Stephanie gestured acquiescence with her hands.

It was awkward but not impossible for Jacinta to see what was happening, a task not made easier by the girl's baggy undies. At least the baby wouldn't rush out at great speed with all that cotton around him or her, Jacinta thought wryly.

'Your baby is coming feet first and there's a little bottom sitting there on the outside. We'll get you into the hospital and see about meeting the rest of your baby in a more comfortable place. What do you think?'

Stephanie gave a strangled laugh of relief as she agreed.

'Good girl. Can you climb out backwards, maybe slither along on your bottom and we'll get you inside so we can see what's going on?'

'I'm scared to move. Here comes another pain.'

'I know. Breathe through it. You're doing fine. But we need to get you inside and the maternity staff are coming. I bet your baby would much prefer to be born on clean sheets.' She heard a fervent agreement from behind her head and realised the cabbie was still there.

Jacinta grinned to herself, then turned her head and nodded to the nurse to push the wheelchair closer to the car. She put her arms around the young woman and as soon as the contraction finished together they inched out of the car.

The next five minutes saw the obstetrician arrive at the same time as the baby was fully born. Jacinta had been calmly waiting for the tiny nape of baby's neck to descend into sight, and as she allowed gravity to do the tricky traction of a breech delivery, she couldn't help but remember the breech births she'd shared with Jonah. The birth was beautiful but the tears in Jacinta's eyes were for another time and place.

Soon Stephanie's baby lay safely in her mother's arms and the maternity staff arranged their transfer upstairs. Jacinta stripped off her gloves and dropped the bloodied latex into the bin. She sighed as she elbowed on the taps and soaped her hands and wrists as if to wash away the sadness she was always left with when she thought of Jonah. As she dried her hands her gaze was caught by Jonah's ring. She'd never taken it off.

Three months she'd been back in Australia now, and he was on her mind constantly. Today was no different and she glanced across to the ambulance bay as another stretcher was wheeled in.

One of the nurses signalled to Jacinta and hurriedly she dried her hands and crossed the hallway. Her footsteps slowed until she came to a complete stop and stared down at the familiar face. Her mind must be playing tricks because she'd been thinking of him.

Sweat trickled in tiny rivulets down his forehead past the rock-solid angles of his cheekbones and pooled in the crevices of his muscular neck.

Titanic rigors shook the white sheet sideways off his body and Jacinta noted the rapid rise and fall of his solid chest which seemed to stretch across the bed when she replaced the covering. She raised her finger and touched his face. He felt real.

'You OK, Doctor?' The ambulance officer's concern was clear in his voice and Jacinta turned blindly towards him.

'Jonah is here?' Her words seemed to come from a long way off. The room darkened all of a sudden and Jacinta had strange trouble focusing her eyes on the man in front of her. Her breath caught in her throat and her next words were a whisper.

The ambulance officer checked his chart. 'His wallet says his name is Jonah Armstrong.'

'I'm sorry. I don't understand. I was told Jonah died in Papua New Guinea in March at the hands of rebels.'

'I don't know anything about that. This guy was picked up from a house in Bondi.'

The words echoed eerily around in Jacinta's mind and the last thing she saw was the concerned face of the ambulance officer as she collapsed bonelessly to the floor.

When she woke up she was on a stretcher, and one of the nurses was sitting beside her. The administrator was hovering anxiously above her.

She felt sick. 'What happened?'

'You fainted. The nurses say you've been doing too much. Go home and rest.'

Then she remembered Jonah. 'Is it true that Jonah Armstrong is here? Alive?'

The administrator nodded. 'I've asked and apparently that is so. You've had a shock and are in no state to see him, neither is he well enough for visitors.'

The administrator helped her sit up and her head swam as the blood drained from her face. 'Go home, Jacinta. One of the nurses will drive you and come back in a taxi. I'll phone you when your Mr Armstrong is well enough to see you.'

Jacinta had thought he was 'her' Mr Armstrong. She sighed and swung her legs gingerly over the side of the bed. Obviously he wasn't.

That Jonah was alive was unbelievable, wonderful. But she didn't understand. Why hadn't Jonah contacted her? What possible reason could there be for him to not even let her know he was alive? After what they had been through together! Her thoughts circled and dipped and her head ached.

She followed the nurse out to her car. Did Jonah assume she knew he was safe now? Did he think she'd left him there to die? It was all too much to comprehend.

Tucked up in bed after her colleague had fussed around her and finally left her in peace, Jacinta tried to make sense of why Jonah hadn't contacted her. How could he possibly have decided she wouldn't be worried?

All she could come up with was that he regretted the exact thing that Jacinta could never regret—their solemn marriage vows. That and the fact that they'd made love—and that he'd said he loved her and would spend the rest of his life with her—must have weighed too heavily on him once they were both safe. Which presented the problem of her pregnancy.

Her hand crept protectively over her stomach, and to her disgust weak tears spilled down her cheeks. Her boss was right. She must have gone back too early because she'd never been this indecisive in her life.

A heavy inertia settled over her and a wave of dark weariness forced her to slide down into the bed. She'd sleep for an hour and her head would be clearer. If

Jonah was as sick as the first time she'd seen him, it would be useless to see him until tomorrow anyway.

The shining light in this mess was that Jonah was alive!

Jonah was gripped by the fever. His skin felt as if he was slowly being roasted over a fire and every muscle ached. Glimpses of Melinda and the woman he called Angel seemed to float through his mind, and he ached with remorse that he'd let them both down. Flashes of his trek through the jungle mixed with an urgency to find somebody missing made his body twist and turn on the bed, but he could never grasp the gossamer identity of the person he'd lost.

When he woke late the next morning, any sense had evaporated from his dreams and the aches in his muscles had faded a little so that he could attempt to sit up.

A quiet knock at his door heralded a visitor, and he turned his head gingerly to see who entered.

A dark-browed young woman stood in the doorway, and he thought she looked so pale she appeared on the verge of shock. Maybe it was only because she had such dark hair and dark eyes against her pale skin. She froze when he lifted his chin in enquiry and to his surprise tears began to trickle down her cheeks until she dashed them away impatiently.

'Can I help you?' His voice croaked with dryness.

When she didn't answer he tried to make sense of her visit but he was just too tired. He leaned back against the pillows. 'Have you come to the wrong room?'

'No. This is the right room.' She drew in a shaky breath and straightened her shoulders as if steeling herself for an unpleasant task.

A suspicion formed in his mind that perhaps the last person who had been in this bed had died and she hadn't known.

'I'm sorry, but do I know you?' He felt inadequate but she wasn't his problem.

The woman lifted her chin as if annoyed with herself and maybe him, too, then drew her magnificent brows together to frown at him. 'My name is Jacinta McCloud and we spent two days kidnapped together in Papua New Guinea in March.'

His confusion lifted. 'Ah. March. I apologise. So you are Dr McCloud.' He frowned when she flinched at her name, confused by the mixed signals she was sending. What was going on here? 'I had planned to visit you while I was in Sydney because I hoped you might be able to fill in some gaps.' He gestured wryly to the bed. 'Unfortunately malaria waits for no man.'

She narrowed her eyes and focused on his words. 'What did you mean, ''Ah, March''?'

'March, along with January and February, appears to be missing from my memory. Apparently I sustained a severe blow to the head during my...' he looked up at her and smiled '...our kidnapping, and I remember nothing much since Christmas. I'm so pleased to finally meet you.'

He sat forward again, held out his hand and pre-

tended he didn't feel as weak as a kitten. She crossed
the room and let her small hand rest in his palm. The
physical touch of her warmed him in a place that had
been cold for too long. This was becoming stranger
by the minute.

'Rest, Jonah.' The way she said his name rustled
like a breeze against his memory but before he could
pin down the thought she gently pushed him back
against the pillows.

'I'm so happy to see you.' She bit her lip and swallowed and he realised she was quite emotional about
their meeting. 'But I can see this isn't the time,' she
said. 'Perhaps when you are discharged I could visit
you or you could come to my home.'

'I'd like that.' He hesitated. 'Have I been to your
house before?'

She smiled and he could have watched her for ever
as some memory lit her face. He felt his own lips
curve in response. He was drawn irresistibly to this
woman so maybe the blankness of his memory was
lightening. It certainly seemed worthwhile to follow
her up as a possible means of prodding his subcon-
scious.

'You've been to my house briefly, just once. We'll
arrange it all later. Just get well.' Then she left, with
her back straight and her head high.

Jonah stared at the closed door and his heart
pounded, but he didn't know why. He couldn't remember her face but there was something about her
voice that called to those deep memories he was only
allowed glimpses of.

She was beautiful in an arresting way, and he wondered if he'd been tempted to make a pass at her while they'd been in Papua New Guinea. He hoped not because it would be dreadful bad manners not to remember that. That they had actually made love never crossed his mind.

Jonah sighed and a wave of tiredness engulfed him. This was becoming more complicated than he'd bargained for.

CHAPTER NINE

JACINTA heard the doorbell and her heart skipped at what felt like twice her usual rate. She relived that first feel of her hand in Jonah's yesterday at the hospital—the touch that had proved he wasn't a dream.

Then the solid feel of his chest under her fingers that had allowed the joy to burst through her and believe the reality of his survival.

She hadn't slept but it was as if a huge stone cemented with guilt and grief had been lifted from her shoulders and scattered into a thousand pieces. She felt weightless and giddily excited when, in fact, the hardest part was still to come.

How would she tell Jonah she was pregnant with their baby when he didn't even remember meeting her? What of the details of making love in some makeshift tent when they'd both thought they were going to die, of their secret marriage—did she describe that?

What if he thought she was tricking her or trapping him into something he didn't want? The negatives began to cram her mind and she shook her head and picked up the pace of her footsteps again that she had unconsciously slowed with her fears.

When she opened the door his finger was raised to

press the buzzer again. 'Hello, Jonah,' she said, and his hand froze in the act.

He looked up and she smiled because it was so wonderful to see him alive. He looked a little startled by the warmth of her greeting, and the last thing she wanted to do was scare him away. She bit her lip.

'I'm glad to see you because I thought you were dead.' She felt obliged to enlighten him then shook her head at his confusion, gave up and gestured him in. 'Make yourself at home. I'll explain it all in a minute.'

She watched him pass into the house and she could see he didn't remember having been here before. He looked so tall and dear and she just wanted to feel him wrap her in his arms and tell her it had all been a bad dream—but she was beginning to see that the bad dream hadn't finished yet.

For him there was no 'magic time' between them, no memories, no chance of happily ever after, and suddenly she didn't know what to do.

When he stopped in the middle of the entry she passed him and went ahead. 'This way.' She struggled to keep her voice normal. 'We'll sit in the den. Would you like something to drink?'

'Water would be good.' He sat where he'd sat once before and she poured him a glass from the tray she'd prepared when she'd been killing time, waiting for his arrival.

She began tentatively. 'Does it upset you to talk about your memory loss?'

Jonah shook his head. 'It's a relief. Not many people are interested. I was frustrated at first but we were so busy at Pudjip there was no opportunity to worry about it.

'Obviously the head injury caused a problem, but with the continued gap in my memory they tell me I could be subconsciously repressing memories because I fear them and may never get that period of memory back.'

He glanced at from under his brows. 'Do you know of anything that I could be trying to forget?'

Jacinta didn't know what to say. The time they had been captive had not been pleasant, but she could think of no instance that would be so horrific for Jonah that he would fear its memory—unless it was the fact that they had fallen in love.

Her stomach sank and she tried to keep her voice level. 'Not that I can think of, but then, you were the one carrying the load of our escape and who knew exactly how precarious our existence was for a while there. The horror for me was when I was told you were dead by Mimi, the old woman who saved me.'

He sat forward at that. 'The old woman was a common denominator. I guess she's the one who saved me, too. But then she disappeared once she'd led me to the compound gate.'

He shook his head at all the loose ends. 'You said you thought I'd been killed. How is it that no one told you I came out of the jungle the day after you left for Australia?'

Jacinta clasped one hand with the other to stop herself from fidgeting. 'I suppose there wasn't the opportunity. I came straight back to Australia—couldn't get out of Papua fast enough when I thought you had died—and my father and stepmother came down and took me up the coast to Burra for a while.'

She shuddered. 'I guess Missions Pacific thought I knew. It has been a terrible few months. If I had known of your escape I would have been back on that plane so fast they would have missed me in customs.'

'Why?'

She stared at him and a tense silence stretched between them. *Because I love you. Because I would have wanted to be there for you and for myself.* She didn't say either of those things. Instead, she looked down into her own glass as if the future was there.

Slowly she listed the secondary reasons she would have returned. 'I felt guilty. Responsible for leaving. Mimi bundled me away and I should have made sure there was nothing I could do for you before I left. I wanted to go back but she kept saying you'd been killed and that they had already taken your clothes.'

The memory of that ghastly moment made her shudder and she hoped he'd understand. She looked up at him apologetically.

He smiled wryly. 'That part was true. I woke up in my birthday suit. And she was right.'

He reached across and took her hand. 'We did have more chance separately.'

He stroked her fingers and she stared down at his hand holding hers. She didn't think he realised he was doing it. The tears welled up and she closed her eyes tightly to hold them back.

She would not beg him to remember that he'd said he loved her or that he'd held her hand as they'd recited their vows. But, oh, how she wanted to.

Jacinta pulled her hand free and stood up, then she walked away to face out the window overlooking the road, surreptitiously wiping her eyes. 'So, do they say you'll ever get your memory back?'

The creak of the lounge told her he'd followed her and then his hand was warm on her shoulder and he turned her to face him.

'Apparently, the longer I wait the less likely it is that it will happen.' He lowered his voice as if afraid of the answer. 'Is there anything else I should know?'

'Nothing important.' Her voice faltered and she smiled brightly and stepped back to hold out her right hand.

'I'm sorry I couldn't help bring back your memory.'

Jonah felt disorientated. So that was it. He looked down at her small hand and then took her slim fingers in his own. It was too hard to walk away from her.

There was more to this and he could feel it but not pinpoint it. Almost unconsciously, instead of shaking her hand he used his purchase on her fingers to pull her back towards him slowly until she was warm against his chest.

'I'll have to get used to not having those memories, I guess.' He tightened his grip so she couldn't pull away. 'What if my memory needs jogging?'

They stared at each other and the moment lengthened as each of them tried to see into the other's mind. When he bent down and kissed her, she sighed.

For Jonah, the moment his lips touched hers he was transported back to another time with Jacinta in his arms. He closed his eyes and wrapped his arms around her and lifted her closer until her toes left the floor and she was crushed against him.

Even that wasn't close enough. Her mouth invited and the kiss deepened and he forgot where or why he was anywhere as he breathed in the scent and the taste of the woman in his arms. And she answered him with a longing that touched the core of him with a feeling of homecoming.

Finally their lips parted and he lowered her slowly until she could step back. When he looked into her eyes he saw her tears, and his finger rose to brush them away as they fell on her cheek.

'We've kissed before.' There was no doubt in his statement and she didn't deny it, but she stepped away further and the back of her hand rested across her mouth where he'd left his imprint. He could tell she was struggling with her emotions.

She wasn't the only one. He wanted to pull her into his arms and do that all over again, and more.

His mind raced and there was only one way his thoughts could go which would explain a lot in her reactions.

'Were we lovers?' His voice was harsher than he'd intended and she flinched at the baldness of the question.

From the first time in the hospital he'd known she

was no shrinking flower. Jacinta raised her chin.
'Yes!'

He glanced down at her body as if to remember,
and his gaze lingered on the slight roundness of her
stomach and generous breasts. Before he could say
anything she spun away to the window again.

'I think you'd better go.'

He blinked and realised how crass he'd been. 'Forgive me, Jacinta. Dr McCloud.' He shook his head
and stared at her spine, ramrod straight, ensuring the
distance between them.

This must be hard for her, too. What a coil. She
was right. He should go because there was a lot to
think about.

'May I call again?'

She sighed. 'I don't know. Yes. No. Just go.'

This whole mess was nowhere near finished and he
would return. 'I'll phone you tomorrow morning.' She
didn't answer and he left her standing there with her
back to him.

Jacinta heard his footsteps fading and the tears ran
down her cheeks. She dashed them away angrily. She
hated this weakness the pregnancy had brought her
to.

She hated this whole insecure part of her life and
the feeling that she wasn't in control but at the mercy
of some fickle god who hadn't decided what he was
going to do with them.

She who prided herself on controlling her life. She
couldn't blame Jonah and it certainly wasn't her fault,

but she did need to decide on her course of action in telling Jonah about their baby.

And her father and Noni.

She sighed.

For Jonah there was little sleep that night and he tossed in his bed and remembered the confusion and pain in Jacinta's eyes. He hated to think that he'd caused her distress. Maybe it would be better if he just left her in peace and returned to Pudjip.

But something was holding him back from doing that. In the brief snatches of rest Jonah's dreams were the worst they'd been. As he ran through the jungle, the branches slapped him and snakes darted away from his feet as twisted tree roots tried to catch his ankles. It was raining and he was cold and he could hear a woman's screams, but he couldn't find her. He ran this way and that as he tried to find her, but the cries didn't seem any closer. He had to find her before something terrible happened, but then it was too late. Her screams were cut off and he sat bolt upright in bed and realised it had been a nightmare.

His hand shook as he reached across and took a sip of water to clear the ache in his throat. When he sat on the edge of the bed his heart pounded in his chest.

Jacinta was the key. She could help him remember. He knew she could. He'd never felt closer than he'd been that day to remembering. Maybe when he saw her tomorrow he'd remember more.

Now that he knew they'd been lovers, there were

more questions. Had they had a relationship in
Sydney, in Pudjip or when they were kidnapped?

How could he not remember that? How had he
come to allow her to follow him to PNG where the
dangers were too great for a woman like her? If they
had been lovers, surely they'd taken precautions? All
very serious questions that he needed to ask. And
what had he been thinking to become involved?

He wandered up to the turret room of a house he
didn't remember buying and stared out at the moonlight shining on the ocean. He spun the telescope and
stared out to sea. Damn this memory loss. He hated
not having control over a situation, and this was so
far out of his grasp he just had to go along for the
ride. Maybe tomorrow would bring answers.

Jacinta woke late because it had taken her so long to
get to sleep. The impact of being in Jonah's arms
again had swept her feet out from under her and she
wasn't sure how she was going to manage if he decided he didn't want to have anything to do with her
or their child—but manage she would have to.

The decision to fight had come during the night.
She would fight for what they had because, through
no fault of either of them, they were in danger of
losing something that only came along once in a lifetime.

She would tell him that she loved him and that he
had said that he loved her. She would tell of their
time in the camp and, depending on his response to

that, she would decide whether to tell him about their child.

But when he was facing her outside her door later that morning, the precariousness of their future frightened the life out of her. What if he had never loved her?

Standing on her doorstep, so tall and dear but so different, today he was determined and the purpose in his face made her wonder what decision he'd come to.

'I've thought about what happened yesterday and I have a few questions.' Jonah took a step forward and now that the moment had come she wasn't sure she was ready for decisions. As she debated whether to let him in, he capitalised on her indecision and stepped past her.

She followed him warily as he led the way to her den and he waited beside his chair for her to sit down first.

Jacinta sighed and sank into the chair opposite. 'We'll see.'

He was frowning as he tried to pin down the elusive background to their relationship and she felt sorry for him again.

'You don't strike me as the sort of woman who enters relationships easily, so if we've made love then you must have had reasons for doing so.'

Jacinta wondered if he realised how offensive he sounded. She shook her head and forgave him because she knew that the real Jonah would never intentionally hurt anyone. 'Thank you for that assessment of my character and, yes, I had my reasons.'

'I'm sorry. That sounded bad.' He looked a little shamefaced and she brushed his apology aside with an airy hand. At least he went on with more diffidence. 'So I guess what I'm trying to find out is— were we in a relationship in Sydney?'

This she could answer. 'No. We barely knew each other. I looked after you in January when you had the first attack of malaria and you rang me a week later to look at a house with you.'

'Ah. The missing house. I only found the house because my solicitor had left a message at Pudjip about that. What intrigues me is why I would ask someone I barely knew to look at real estate with me.'

Jacinta raised her eyebrows. 'And your point is?'

'Why did I ask you?'

She couldn't see how this would help but she humoured him. 'You said it was because when you looked at houses on your own, you felt that the owners were more comfortable if you had a woman with you.'

She raised her eyebrows again, sceptically this time. 'I think it was a line, Dr Armstrong. A little like, come and see my etchings. We looked at the house, came back here for coffee and that was the last time I saw you before you met me in Hagen a month or so later.'

'So there was no relationship in Sydney.'

'As I've said.'

His eyes narrowed. 'What about Pudjip?'

'Pudjip was work.' She remembered some of the special moments they'd shared and the gradual build-up of rapport between them. Did a kiss constitute a relationship? 'There was no relationship in Pudjip.'

He sat back in his chair. 'Which leaves the time we were kidnapped.'

Jacinta avoided his eyes. 'As for the circumstances of our abduction, the danger in our situation certainly precipitated things before we really knew each other.'

He nodded impatiently. 'I can understand that, but we must have been drawn to each other before that. Perhaps if we began to know each other now, those feelings would come back and with the feelings my memory would come back.'

He looked quite excited about the prospect, but Jacinta was more wary.

Jonah was oblivious. 'Tell me about your life, your childhood. Something should trigger what it was that we found.'

Jacinta tilted her head and looked at him thoughtfully. 'That's fairly in-depth stuff. What are you going to tell me in exchange?'

He spread his hands as if to say he had nothing to hide. 'What do you want to know?'

Jacinta ticked the points off on her fingers. 'About your sister and how she died. About your life growing up as a missionary child. About what you've been doing the last three months.'

He shrugged that off and she smiled at the way he avoided talking about himself. 'Was it because you thought you loved me that we made love?'

Her smile died from her face and she drew a deep breath before she met his eyes. How to answer?

She remembered the bravery of Jonah's declaration in the tent the night before she'd escaped and his fearless admission about loving her. How could those memories not give her strength? Her resolve firmed and she looked up.

'I didn't "think" I loved you—I did grow to love the man I was abducted with. But there is some safety in there for you, too, because the last thing I want to do is make you unhappy. If that man has changed and doesn't love me now, or won't grow to love me, then I would expect you to go.' She tilted her chin. 'Despite what we found together in those last few hours.'

He sighed and shook his head. 'Thank you for your honesty.'

Jacinta could feel the tension in her shoulders and she knew she'd avoided the main reason.

He tilted his head. 'So why do I think there is something you're not telling me?' The man was like a terrier.

She glanced down at the table. 'I don't know. What makes you think there is?'

'You've been incredibly open about your feelings, but I know there's something else.'

Again she looked away.

'See,' he said. 'That's just what I mean. You're open and honest, and when you avoid a subject you look away.'

'Maybe I'm bored?'

'Or lying?'

Jacinta could feel her control slipping. They were going nowhere. She really didn't think she could stand any more dissection of her suffering. 'I think you'd better leave. I've tried to be honest and you've given me nothing to believe that I've laid myself open for good reason.'

'I'm sorry, Jacinta. I know this must be hard for you.' He ran his hand through his hair. 'For me, I'm thirty-seven years old and never intended to hurt you. I don't understand how I could let it get so far. I'm too old to change my ways. I love my job and it's too dangerous to have a family. I'm used to travelling light.'

His voice dropped but what he said was very clear. 'I promised, when my sister died, that I would never risk another woman's life because she loved me and wanted to be with me. I don't know what I was thinking during our capture, but at this moment I must stand by beliefs I've held for ten years. There's no future in a relationship between us.'

So that's it, then. Jacinta closed her eyes for an agonised minute to gather her thoughts. It was no more or less than she'd told herself in the tent all those weeks ago.

She reminded herself that she loved this man, but he didn't love her enough to risk his own pain if anything happened to her. This fiasco was going from bad to worse.

Her stomach reacted in protest. She needed some food for her churning stomach and her head had be-

gun to ache. Either way, she couldn't face Jonah
Armstrong any more at this moment.

Jacinta closed her eyes briefly and allowed her
shoulders to droop. Then she opened her eyes for one
last look at him. She tugged at the signet ring he'd
given her. 'This is yours.'

His eyes widened. 'How did you get that? I thought
the men had stolen it when they took my clothes.'

She looked away. 'You gave it to me for safekeep-
ing. Perhaps you could show yourself out.'

Jacinta left him standing there and ran up the stairs
to the safety of her room where she shut the door and
leaned against it. She was a mess, mentally and physically, and Jonah had only made it worse. She wanted
Noni and her father. She wanted her family around
her and distance between her and Jonah and freedom
from decisions that she didn't know were right or
wrong.

Jonah walked down Jacinta's front steps and stared
at the ring. It was still warm from her finger. He was
glad to be outside because suddenly his head thumped
with pain and he felt sick. His sister's ring cut into
his palm as he clenched his fist and tried to control
his nausea.

He drove home carefully, crawled into bed and
pulled the covers over his head to block out the light.
He hoped like hell he wasn't coming down with malaria again—though it didn't feel like that.

These symptoms were different, and the pain increased until he screwed up his face and moaned.
Then everything went black.

When he surfaced hours later, Jonah was so close to remembering that he didn't want to return to reality and fought against waking up. Suddenly it was as if Jacinta was there and she slid her hands down against his chest and he just wanted her skin against his. 'You are so beautiful,' he murmured as his lips brushed one creamy shoulder.

'Make love to me, Jonah. So I can know that you are real and we are both really here.'

She reached for him and then they were both naked and together on the thick carpet, Jacinta in his arms, her skin like silk, soft against his chest.

He rolled over onto his back, bringing her with him, until she stared down at him and he could drink in the sight of her, with her black hair hanging each side of her face and her dark eyes burning into his.

He reached up to cup her face but suddenly she was gone again.

There was no one above him and when he opened his eyes he realised she was the angel of his dreams.

The pain in his head had eased but the one in his heart had grown. Even though his memory had not returned, he knew Jacinta was everything he wanted in a woman and everything he refused to risk.

Many hours later, when he finally slept again, he dreamt of the horror of Melinda's death and in the morning he knew his decision to leave had been the right one.

Jonah woke with the sun. His headache a dull reminder now, he swung his feet to the floor and waited for the giddiness to pass before he turned his head to glance at the clock.

It was early yet, but she'd probably be up. His hand paused as he pulled on his shoes. He wondered if she'd even talk to him because he'd almost worn his welcome out the last time he'd seen her. He needed to tell her he would return to Pudjip. He owed that much to her.

The drive to Jacinta's house took less time than it should have, but there were no signs of life in the house. When he rang the doorbell nobody answered.

Jonah stepped back and tried to see inside the windows, but they all seemed to be shut with blinds drawn.

Had she gone away or was she pretending she wasn't there? He mocked himself for the thought. She wasn't the type to cower behind curtains and pretend absence. Jacinta had gone away to escape him and it was for the best. He returned to his car and drove home to pack his bags for Pudjip.

CHAPTER TEN

WHEN Jacinta climbed out of the car after the six-hour drive to Burra, Iain McCloud, his wife Noni and Noni's Aunt Win were all there to greet her.

'Hello, Jaz. Welcome home.' Her father dropped a kiss on the top of her head, Noni reached up to hug her and Aunt Win folded her in her arms and spun her around. Jacinta realised she'd come to the right place.

'It's good to be here.' They ushered her inside and Jacinta could feel the tension easing away from her neck. This time she felt seventeen again and accepted that others would care for her until she could recoup her stamina. Her shoulders slumped with pleasant weariness and she sank into the chair in the study. It was so good to have her family around her.

'You need rest and fattening up, young woman.' Aunt Win had taken one look at her and given her usual diagnosis.

Jacinta met Noni's eyes around the elderly lady's not inconsiderable girth and smiled. Aunt Win was known for trying to fatten people up and she bustled away, no doubt to fetch a laden teatray.

Iain and Noni sat together on the lounge and Iain draped his arm around his wife's shoulders and absently stroked her arm with his fingers.

Since their marriage twelve years ago, Iain's adoration of his second wife had only grown.

Jacinta couldn't help a trickle of self-pity when she thought of what it would mean to have Jonah sit in such a way with her.

Aunt Win returned and Iain jumped up to take the tray and set it down for her. Noni leaned forward to pour the tea, and when the four of them were settled she looked across at Jacinta. 'Now that Aunt Win is here, tell us how you are.'

Jacinta sighed back in the chair. 'I'm tired and confused and I don't know which way to go, so I thought I'd come home for a day or two to sort out my head.'

There was a small silence and Noni went on quietly, 'You made the right choice to come home. It was wonderful news that Jonah escaped as well. We couldn't believe it when you rang us. You said you were going to see him. How does he look?'

'He looks well.' She looked down into her cup. 'Fabulous, actually.' Noni and Iain exchanged a look that Jacinta didn't see and she went on, 'But he's suffered a head injury and lost the last three months of his memory before the kidnap. So he doesn't remember me or the time we were kidnapped.'

Iain's interest sharpened. 'Focal amnesia, eh?' He chose a plump brown scone and bit into it, and didn't see the warning look his wife sent him. 'Tricky and possibly permanent. Usually to block out a particular incident or fear.'

'Obviously you're interested in the technical side, darling.' Noni and Aunt Win glared at him.

He caught the tail end of his wife's displeasure and raised his eyebrows. 'What?'

But Noni had turned back to Jacinta.

'It must have been hard for you when you first saw him.' Noni's voice was gentle and Aunt Win leaned across and squeezed Jacinta's knee.

Noni smiled sideways at her husband. 'Most people get their memory back, don't they, Iain?'

Not slow to take a hint, Iain agreed. 'Often a mirror incident or visual or aural trigger can help. Is he having flashbacks?'

Jacinta sighed. 'I don't know. If I see him again I'll ask him.' She swallowed the lump in her throat. 'Though I might not see him again.' She opened her mouth to say something else but looked at her father and clamped her lips shut.

Noni winked at her husband and jerked her head towards the door. He raised his eyebrows as if to say, *I don't understand*, and Noni pretended to glare. Iain grinned and stood up.

'Excuse me, Jaz. I've remembered I need to make a phone call. I'll be back in a minute.'

He squeezed his daughter's shoulder and Aunt Win stood up as well.

'Just going to put tonight's meal on,' she said to no one in particular, and Noni smiled.

Jacinta looked at Noni and grimaced. 'That was subtle.'

'Your father doesn't know subtle.' Noni patted the seat beside her. 'Come and sit over here, Jaz.'

Jacinta moved across and sank onto the lounge be-

side Noni, who put her arm around her. 'There is
more to this than you told us last time you were here.'
Noni hugged Jacinta who leaned into her and rested
her head as she dashed a hand across her eyes.

'I'm a grown woman. I'm acting like a clueless
teenager, but I love Jonah so much it hurts.'

She looked at Noni, and her stepmother nodded. 'I
remember that all too well.'

'I knew you'd understand. We fell in love while
we were kidnapped. Well…' She qualified the statement. 'It grew from the first moment we saw each
other. He said that, too, and now his memory of it all
is gone.'

'Oh, my love. You poor thing. Does he remember
anything about the two of you?'

'He remembered he'd kissed me before when he
kissed me yesterday.'

Noni smiled gently. 'That sounds promising.'

Jacinta gave a bitter little laugh. 'That's what I
thought. But it's not enough.' She turned her head
and looked at Noni. 'Especially as I'm pregnant.'

Noni pursed her lips and squeezed Jacinta's hand.
'Does he know?'

Jacinta shook her head and Noni sighed. 'Another
dilemma. You poor old sausage.'

She hugged Jacinta again. 'This is too much for
you right now. You are incredible to be still standing
up after the three months you've had. Forget everything for tonight. I'll hold all of your problems here.'
She tapped her chest. 'And you will sleep and rest

and eat for twenty-four hours. Then we will see what happens when you have your reserves back.'

'How can I do that?' Jacinta sat up and squared her shoulders as if to take up her burdens again.

'Get sleep. You know we do the same for those poor mothers who have problems settling their babies and they come into Maternity Ward totally exhausted and not knowing which way to turn. Forget your troubles briefly.'

Jacinta rolled her eyes. 'I don't have breastfeeding problems, Noni!'

'You're sleep-deprived and stressed. Don't worry at your problems because they will all still be there when you get back from your time out. They'll just be more manageable and you won't be alone. We'll all be here for you and your head will be clearer.'

Jacinta shook her head fondly at her stepmother. 'It does sound wonderful.'

'It's done. Now, go upstairs and lie down. I'll wake you for tea because we want you to sleep tonight as well. Later, Harley will want to show you his new purple car now that he's seventeen with his driver's licence, and Nanette will be excited when she finds out you're home.'

They both stood up and Jacinta hugged Noni. 'Thank you. You are the best stepmother in the world.'

'Wicked.' Noni said Harley's favourite word and they both laughed.

Iain clenched his fist. 'So what's this fellow's name? What sort of missionary doctor is he anyway, getting my daughter pregnant while she does volunteer work?' Iain took a turn around the room and Noni watched him let off steam without saying a word.

'Can't he see she's struggled so hard to get where she is today? Now she's back at the beginning again.'

'No, she's not.' Noni judged the time was right to have her say. 'Jacinta is a capable career-woman and we know she can be an excellent mother. If she and Jonah don't end up together, she will manage beautifully. The fact that she loves a man who doesn't know he loves her is the problem.'

'Jonah!' Iain scowled. 'He's *Jonah'd* my daughter, that's what he's done.'

Noni laughed softly and stood up and planted her feet in her husband's way so that he had to stop pacing. 'Now, remember that the path of true love is often difficult. I don't believe Jacinta would fall in love with an unworthy man. Not as *in love* as she obviously is.' She leaned up and kissed him. 'They are probably as in love as we are even after all these years.'

Iain looked down at his diminutive wife and his face and voice softened. 'Oh, they couldn't be *that* much in love.'

He kissed her back. 'All right. So the guy didn't mean to get amnesia and maybe Jaz consented to sleep with him, but why hasn't he followed her here?'

'He's probably as confused as she is. Give him time. Give them both time. And if he does turn up, I want you to be the charming man I know you can be and not some irate father who's forgotten that his daughter is nearly thirty years old and not seventeen.'

'What would we do without you?'

Noni gave a cheeky grin and turned to leave the room. She looked back. 'I don't know what you would do, but I'd be lost.' She blew her husband a kiss and trotted down the stairs, smiling at the wolf whistle that followed her.

When Jacinta woke the next morning she did feel more in control. Noni arrived with a tray of breakfast for her and then she perched on the side of the bed.

'How do you feel, Jaz?'

'Better. I've decided to go back to Sydney to find Jonah, and if he's gone, I'll follow him to Papua New Guinea. Maybe me being there will help his memory return.'

'And what are you going to tell him when you find him?'

Her voice shook. 'Nothing about our baby yet because it would colour his decision.' Then she strengthened. 'I'm going to do the work I went there to do for the few more weeks I have left before my pregnancy shows, prove that I can handle the life and just be thankful that Jonah isn't dead.' She looked at Noni. 'The rest is up to him.'

'So you'd go back to Papua New Guinea and work again in the hospital? Do you want to do that?' Noni looked at Jacinta searchingly.

'I want to. I loved the work and the people. But I have to come home to Burra to have my baby.'

Noni hugged Jacinta and tears filled their eyes as they both thought of the last tiny baby of Jacinta's that had been born there. 'I can understand why you want to do that.'

'If I get sick, will you make sure I get home?'

Noni smiled. 'I'm sure your father and his friends will make sure of that.'

Jonah heard the Jeep drive in to Pudjip and his hand froze in the act of writing. Jacinta must have pulled some strings because he'd been trying his hardest to keep her in Australia.

He had no idea what Jacinta McCloud's real reason was behind her arrival, only that she'd told Missions Pacific she'd be staying for a month to make up for the time she hadn't completed. He would have to count down the days until the torture was finally over.

The patient chart beneath his fingers seemed to fade as he stared through it as if to see the right path to take.

She was here—the woman he could only remember meeting twice—but whose presence still dominated his thoughts and his dreams. He had no idea how his confusion had come to this and he'd ended up in a situation he'd always sworn he would avoid.

A few minutes later her quiet footsteps entered his tiny office and he put the pen down.

'Hello, Jonah.' Jacinta's voice drifted across the room to him like a siren's call, and slowly he lifted his chin to face her.

She was even more beautiful than he remembered.

Or maybe she was just beautiful to him. Her dark eyes seemed to see right through him and the determination in her face told him there was nothing he could say to make her leave before she decided to. Finally he accepted she would see out her term and it was up to him to keep her safe.

'Dr McCloud.' He stood up and she crossed the room to shake his hand. He hesitated but she stood in front of him with hand outstretched and he had no choice. Ah, Jacinta, he thought, you don't know how dangerous this is. He sighed. Her fingers were warm and wonderful beneath his.

'You look well,' he said. And she did. Her cheeks glowed pink and her black hair shone lustrously in the poor light of his office. She'd gained a little weight and even her breasts looked rounder. He dragged his eyes away from her body to the doorway behind her to ground himself.

He needed her outside this room because in this relative privacy he was tempted to recapture the elusive magic he'd felt that day in her house with his arms around her and his lips against hers. Since returning to Pudjip it had been even harder than he'd feared to put aside the few memories he did have of Jacinta.

He straightened. The only solution was to treat her like any other volunteer. 'I'll show you around and where you'll sleep.'

'I *have* been here before, Jonah,' she said quietly, and he realised that, of course, that was true.

'Then come and say hello to Carla and Samuel.'

She followed him as he left the office, and he breathed a sigh of relief until she laughed softly.

'That's funny,' she said from behind his shoulder. 'Samuel told me it was you who asked him to pick me up.'

He'd forgotten the arrangements he'd put in place for her arrival, and he couldn't blame the amnesia. The woman made him crazy in a way he'd never been crazy before.

The best thing he could do was put her to work. There was always enough of that.

Jacinta followed him and for the moment she was content to just settle in. The sight of him, so tall and vital, soothed the part of her that still woke sweating with memories of when she'd thought he'd died. He seemed a little distracted and she wondered if her arrival had unsettled him. She hoped so.

She hung back a little just to savour the sight of his strong shoulders and broad back, which she remembered so vividly beneath her hands. The thrill of excitement she'd been trying to keep in check grew in her stomach. He was her man and she had done the right thing to come here to fight for him.

She caught up and as they crossed the ward, Jacinta's gaze rested on a small boy who was wriggling around on his bed like a happy fish, all eyes and wide smile as he tried to catch her attention.

'Peeta!' She left Jonah and swept the little boy into her arms and hugged him. 'You look so big.'

'Me big and muscles.' The boy flexed his skinny arms importantly and Jacinta laughed. She tousled his hair and stood up. 'I come back, quick-quick, you wait.' She'd brought a tiny red fire engine in her luggage from Sydney in case Peeta was back again as an inpatient. It had been the memory of his smiling face that had helped her remember the reason they had been in Papua New Guinea and the life Jonah had chosen.

Over the next few hours Jacinta slipped into the routine as if she'd never left, and she marvelled again at how calm and caring Jonah was with his patients. This was where he belonged. She just needed him to see that she belonged by his side.

Days and then two weeks passed, and she'd graduated into looser tops and baggier pants. She didn't think anyone would notice the tiny bulge that proclaimed her condition, although she had seen Carla nod to herself.

Suddenly she found herself alone with Jonah more often as first Carla and then Samuel seemed to find other things to do when the three or four of them ended up working together. Once she caught Carla's knowing smile and it felt good to have an ally or two.

Gradually Jonah softened, as she knew his fairness would make him do. They shared a few jokes and he soon began to meet her eyes at crucial moments in patient care as if to share the burden with her. That was why she was here. Not just for herself and her baby but because Jonah needed to share the weight of his responsibilities. But he didn't say anything. It was as if the evolution of his feelings was happen-

ing without his consent and he refused to acknowledge them.

By the third week they were at stalemate. Jacinta
loved him more than ever and she didn't think he was
immune to her, but she began to fear he would never
change his mind.

His reservations for her safety would never allow
her to stay, and she began to wonder if she had the
right to force him. The last days passed swiftly and
the distance Jonah had placed between them remained
as unbreachable as it had been when Jacinta had first
arrived, at least on the outside.

Jacinta's dilemma was her pregnancy. She hadn't
wanted to influence Jonah's decision with such a
weapon, but now that she had little hope he would
ask her to stay it was his right to know he was to be
a father before she left. The right moment to share
her news never seemed to materialise. The day before
she left finally dawned and she could wait no longer.

For Jonah, it was the day before the one he dreaded
and a day he longed for. She seemed everywhere.
Even without the earlier memories, she infiltrated his
thoughts as he worked and he knew he had to make
her leave before he weakened and took her in his arms
again. There seemed so much magic associated with
Jacinta as he watched her work. He had to keep reminding himself that his way had always been alone,
that the events of March only highlighted the danger
to her and strengthened his resolve.

All he could do was try not to be alone with her.
Like this morning. Carla and Samuel stood up as he

entered the communal dining room and again they left the two of them to eat together.

There was something different about Jacinta today, Jonah thought as he glanced across the table. She seemed nervous or unsettled, and his skin prickled with unease.

'Last day and you'll be back in civilisation.' Jacinta thought his eyes softened when he looked at her but he was talking openly about her impending departure. She needed to break the news to him.

'I need to talk to you, Jonah. It's important. Will you listen now?'

He looked at her and something flickered in his eyes that belied his nod. 'Sure,' he said.

But then Carla rushed in and called him and Jacinta watched him hurry off. She sighed. Maybe tonight would be better.

Another busy day passed. It was going on dusk when the young woman approached the gatekeeper and asked for Missy-Dokkta.

When the message came, Jacinta looked across the ward at Jonah, his head bent over the patient he was talking to, and she wondered if she could slip away without him seeing. He would be livid if he knew she was talking to someone outside the compound.

As she approached the gate she recognised the young mother from the kidnappers' rebel camp.

'Is your baby sick, Neena?'

Neena shook her dark hair. 'Mimi sick. Mimi die if Missy-Dokkta not come.'

Jacinta frowned. 'Bring Mimi to hospital. Much better.'

'Mimi not come till Missy-Dokkta say OK. Not get in trouble.'

'Mimi's not in trouble. Mimi is my friend.' Jacinta shook her head.

'You come tell her that.'

Jacinta shuddered. She wasn't that stupid. 'I'm not going back to Mimi's camp.'

'Meet just little way away. Then Mimi come.'

'I'm not allowed to leave the compound.'

'We be quick-quick.'

'Not that quick, Neena. I ask Dokkta to come and talk to you.'

'No. Dokkta not come. Missy-Dokkta safe.'

The dilemma was real and Jacinta chewed her finger. She could not forget that Mimi had not only saved her life but the life of Jonah as well. Jacinta didn't believe that Neena would cause her harm either. She wanted to help her if she could. If they were quick she could be back before Jonah knew she was gone.

If he discovered she'd left there would be hell to pay. But then a little hell might be worth it because she was sick of this wall of politeness he'd erected.

She went to pack an emergency medical bag.

CHAPTER ELEVEN

'WHERE'S Dr McCloud?' Jonah entered the dining room a little after six and was surprised to see Jacinta's place at the table still vacant. Carla looked up from the bowl of vegetables she was dishing out and glanced around.

She met her husband's eyes and Samuel shrugged denial of any knowledge of Jacinta's whereabouts. 'We thought she was with you.'

Jonah glanced at his watch and his unease deepened. 'I haven't seen her for an hour or so.'

Carla frowned at the concern in his voice. 'She's probably in her hut. I'll go and look for her.'

Jonah shook his head. 'You stay and have your meal. I'll go.'

Jonah stamped down the panic that had appeared out of nowhere. There was no reason for him to think that anything had happened to Jacinta. She was only late for a meal, which was something he was often guilty of.

He checked her room, but there was no answer when he knocked. He knocked again and then went along to check the communal bathroom and the long ward of the hospital. The evening shift hadn't seen her.

Finally he skirted the building and poked his head into the labour ward. Still no sign of Jacinta.

The casualty room was in darkness so she wasn't in there either, and the feeling of unease that was growing inside him brought a cold sweat to his brow.

The walk to the gatehouse was the longest walk of his life. His heart thumped in his chest, and he prayed the whole way that she hadn't left the compound.

When he reached the gatekeeper's hut he pounded on the door with enough force to propel the keeper out of his chair and onto the floor. The little man picked himself up and hurried to the door.

'Have you seen Dr McCloud?'

'Missy-Dokkta left Pudjip with tribal woman one hour ago.'

Jonah felt the gaping chasm of his worst fears open beneath him. 'How did she leave?'

'On foot.'

Just like Melinda.

Suddenly his head split with pain and nausea rose in his throat, as had happened the day Jacinta had given him back the ring. He looked down at his hand and his sister's ring and the butterfly cut into his palm as he clenched his fist and tried to shut out the agony inside his head. But the wave of pain increased until he screwed up his face and moaned. Then everything went black.

When he woke up, the kaleidoscope of the last few months streamed past in his mind with a clarity that stunned him. His trip to Sydney, the malaria and meeting Jacinta, the two of them at his house and even her first arrival in Mt Hagen—all there in Technicolor detail.

He remembered the tense nights of the kidnapping and the final morning after their symbolic marriage, the glory and fear when he'd been sure they would both die that day. Then the kaleidoscope wound down and he lived the next memories second by second.

His heart rate accelerated and cold sweat broke out on his brow again as he relived his terror when Jacinta had left the tent with Mimi the second time.

He hadn't trusted them. It had been too close to sunrise and the promise of death. He'd needed to take Jacinta from there or something bad would be unavoidable.

He'd dug the knife quickly from beneath the post and stepped to the rear of the tent where he'd slit the tough canvas to make a hole big enough to escape through as soon as Jacinta returned. Then the old woman had reappeared without her.

'Dokkta lady want medicines.' Mimi had snatched up the bag and the guard had gestured for Jonah to step back while she'd left the tent.

That was when the guard said he would be having big sport with the dokkta's woman when the sun rose.

Jonah didn't remember how his hands came to be around the throat of the guard, but a searing pain and a flash of light as another guard hit him—he remembered that. Along with the cold shock of realisation he hadn't saved Jacinta. Then nothing, until he awoke beside the tree with the old woman.

Obviously the guards must have thought him dead.

Either way, they had left him, and with Mimi's help he escaped. As had Jacinta.

He twisted in the bed and forced his eyes open. Jacinta, his wife, was out there in the jungle and he needed to find her.

'Can you hear me, Jonah?' Her voice.

He turned his head and there she was. He lifted her fingers to his lips and then pulled her towards him, staring into the eyes of the woman he loved more than life itself. He saw her concern and her love and her fear of rejection again.

Her black hair hung each side of her face like in the dream, and her chest rose and fell with her rapid breathing. She must have hurried to be here. He shook his head at the paleness of her features and sat up on the edge of the bed. 'You're back.'

She smiled. 'Yes. I'll always come back because we are a part of each other.'

'Why did you leave?'

'Some risks must be taken.' She thought of the risk of his anger and that he would still send her away tomorrow if he was unwilling to face his own fears. 'Mimi needed me and now we can look after her like she looked after us.'

'And will you look after me like you have before?'

'Your memory is back?'

He pulled his sister's ring from his finger and it lay in his palm for a moment as they both stared at it. Then he slipped it onto the ring finger of her left hand.

'You remember?' she said, and when her eyes filled with tears he wanted to crush her to him.

'My poor, darling Jacinta.' He pulled her close against his chest and for the first time in months he felt alive. 'I remember everything, and I'm so sorry you had to go through that.' He caught her other hand and her fingers looked so small in his.

'I remember I love you and want to spend the rest of my life with you.'

She stepped back out of his arms and looked up at him. He could see she wanted to believe him, but something was holding her back. 'So what dark and dreadful memory stopped you from remembering that before? Why were you so frightened of remembering me?'

He wasn't proud of his behaviour but she deserved the truth. 'When I discovered you'd left the compound today, the shock and memory of what happened to Melinda shattered the memory block my fears had created.' He sighed.

'That last morning, the closer we came to dawn and the fate in store for us, the closer I came to the memories of how I failed Melinda. I heard them planning to ambush you on the way back with Mimi.' He shook his head and the expression on his face gave him away. 'I had to stop them going for you.' Unconsciously his hands tightened on hers. 'And the last thing I remembered was that I'd failed. I hadn't saved you.'

She'd always known he was more concerned about her fate than his own. It made sense if he believed that she had died a horrible death—just like his sister.

No wonder his mind hadn't allowed him to revisit his worst fears.

Jacinta remembered when he'd said that day in her house that he'd never risk another woman's life because she loved him.

She pulled her hands free and looked up at him, and she knew he could see the indecision in her face. 'How will you cope if we have a family? Where will we live? What about your love of Pudjip? Because if you work here, I'm staying with you.'

He pulled her slowly back against him and stared down into her courageous face. 'A family with you I would adore. You mean everything to me and I can help Pudjip in other ways as well. Missions Pacific have wanted me to lecture for them for years to raise awareness of our plight and need for funds.'

He cupped her cheek in his hand. 'I want to live my life with you. For the last few years I've only existed, and I never dreamt I would find a woman like you. You have such strength and humour and you make me appreciate things I forgot to appreciate years ago.'

Jacinta kissed the hand that lay beside her mouth. 'You would have to let me share responsibility, share your burdens. I won't be left on the outside because I'm your wife.'

He nodded. 'You could give the woman's perspective on medicine in the developing world. You and I could travel the world seeking sponsors, and do occasional stints here at the hospital if that's what we want, or in Sydney.'

'You have it all worked out.'

'Marry me,' he said.

Finally she softened. 'I'm already married.' She smiled as she reached up and kissed him. 'I died inside when I thought you were dead, and it was so hard not to plead with you to love me when you came back and your memory was gone.'

'Let me show you how much I love you.' He looked around at the interested ward and laughed out loud. 'But not here.'

She helped him stand and together they smiled at the caring faces around them.

'Missy-Dokkta now Mrs-Dokkta,' he said mock-seriously to his patients. Then he took her hand as if he would never let her go and they left the ward together.

In his room, he kissed her and wrapped his arms around the woman that he'd never thought would hold him like this again and savoured the softness and vitality that he'd thought were gone for ever.

Later, when they parted, she smiled and looked up into his face. 'And did you suspect I have more news to tell?'

He frowned, his mind sluggish with desire, until her meaning burst into his consciousness. A feeling of awe swept over him and he ran his hand gently over the growing bulge in her stomach.

'My child?'

'Our child.' She leaned up and kissed him. 'Pudjip's child.'

'And what shall we call our baby?'

His face softened as he thought of sharing a new life with his love. 'You choose.'

'We'll have to check with her, but I'd like to call our child Mimi.'

Jonah laughed. 'And if he's a boy?'

'His middle name can be Mimi.'

The wedding was held at Burra and the father of the bride sat down after handing over his daughter.

Iain admired the towering tent his daughter and new son-in-law had hired from the circus, though why they couldn't have had an ordinary marquee he didn't understand. He had to admit, though, that the huge central pole was impressive, with vines that travelled to the roof and luminous stars adorning the apex. But he wasn't sure about the symbolic flower chains that tied the bride and groom together.

'Didn't you see the movie *Braveheart*, Iain?' Noni thought it all very romantic and she squeezed her husband's hand. 'When William Wallace married his lady in the woods with only the preacher?'

Iain lifted his wife's hand to his lips and kissed her palm. 'Must have missed it. Jacinta looks gorgeous, doesn't she?' Iain looked on proudly as his daughter renewed her vows in a voice that carried clearly to the rear of the assembly.

In the centre, Jonah stared down into Jacinta's eyes and remembered another exchange of vows with the same love shining up at him from Jacinta's face. He could barely believe the joy in his heart and the certainty that their life ahead together would be beyond anything he had ever imagined now that he had Jacinta beside him.

With their vows renewed in front of family and friends, Jonah and Jacinta turned to face the congregation. This time light and beauty and new adventures stretched ahead of them and they both embraced their future as they gently kissed.

Then Jonah raised Jacinta's hand and Melinda's signet ring flashed in the light, along with the diamond beside it. 'I introduce you to my wife, Jacinta Armstrong.' His voice was deep and clear and full of pride, and the congregation rose as one and cheered.

As they descended into the throng, Jonah held firmly to his wife's hand. Suddenly two tiny blue butterflies hovered above them in benediction before soaring off into the sunlight.

MILLS & BOON®

Live the emotion

Her Greek Millionaire

Have these gorgeous Greek multimillionaires met their match?

In May 2005, By Request brings back three favourite romances by our bestselling Mills & Boon authors:

The Husband Test *by Helen Bianchin*
The Kyriakis Baby *by Sara Wood*
The Greek Tycoon's Bride
by Helen Brooks

Make sure you get hold of these passionate stories, on sale 6th May 2005

MILLS & BOON®

Volume 11
on sale from
7th May
2005

Lynne
Graham

International Playboys

*A Vengeful
Passion*

0405/01a

MILLS & BOON®

Live the emotion

Modern
romance™

THE ITALIAN'S STOLEN BRIDE by Emma Darcy

Hot-blooded Italian Luc Peretti left Skye Sumner when he thought she'd betrayed him. Six years on Luc learns that Skye was innocent – and that she has borne his son! Skye wants nothing to do with Luc – but Luc won't take no for an answer.

THE PURCHASED WIFE by Michelle Reid

Xander Pascalis can buy anything he wants – including a wife! And though Helen is highly priced, Xander knows she's a good deal. But on their wedding night she refuses to share his bed…

BOUND BY BLACKMAIL by Kate Walker

Jake Taverner wants Mercedes Alcolar. So when she rejects him in the most painful way, his hurt pride demands revenge. Jake traps Mercedes into a fake engagement and embarks on a skilful seduction. But though he can bind her by blackmail…can he keep her?

PUBLIC WIFE, PRIVATE MISTRESS by Sarah Morgan

Only Anastasia, Rico Crisanti's estranged wife, can help his sister. He demands that in public she acts as the perfect wife – but in private she will be slave to his passion. As soon as Rico's sister recovers Stasia fears she will be cast aside. Will her role as Rico's wife be over for good?

Don't miss out…

On sale 6th May 2005

Available at most branches of WHSmith, Tesco, ASDA, Martins, Borders, Eason, Sainsbury's and all good paperback bookshops.

Visit www.millsandboon.co.uk

MILLS & BOON®

Live the emotion

0405/01b

Modern
romance™

AT THE SPANISH DUKE'S COMMAND
by Fiona Hood-Stewart

Georgiana fell for Juan Felipe Mansanto, Duque de Caniza,
even though he was supposed to be her guardian. And it
seemed that, try as he might, Juan couldn't resist her.
But Juan was about to make a marriage of convenience to
another woman...

THE SHEIKH'S VIRGIN *by Jane Porter*

Lots of women have enjoyed the benefits of being Sheikh
Kalen Nuri's mistress – but they have all bored him. Now
Kalen has discovered beautiful Keira – but she's refusing to
be his, even though she has been chosen as his virgin bride!

THE ITALIAN DOCTOR'S MISTRESS *by Catherine Spencer*

Successful neurosurgeon Carlo Rossi has a passion for his
work – and for women. And he desires Danielle Blake like
no other woman. He insists they play by his rules – no
future, just a brief affair. But when it's time for Danielle to
leave Italy can he let her go?

PREGNANT BY THE GREEK TYCOON *by Kim Lawrence*

After a passionate whirlwind marriage to Greek billionaire
Angolos Constantine, Georgie is pregnant. She is sure
Angolos will be delighted – but instead he tells her to go
away and never come back...but he'll have what's his – by
whatever means necessary.

Don't miss out...

On sale 6th May 2005

4 FREE

BOOKS AND A SURPRISE GIFT!

We would like to take this opportunity to thank you for reading this Mills & Boon® book by offering you the chance to take FOUR more specially selected titles from the Medical Romance™ series absolutely FREE! We're also making this offer to introduce you to the benefits of the Reader Service™—

- ★ FREE home delivery
- ★ FREE gifts and competitions
- ★ FREE monthly Newsletter
- ★ Exclusive Reader Service offers
- ★ Books available before they're in the shops

Accepting these FREE books and gift places you under no obligation to buy, you may cancel at any time, even after receiving your free shipment. Simply complete your details below and return the entire page to the address below. You don't even need a stamp!

YES! Please send me 4 free Medical Romance books and a surprise gift. I understand that unless you hear from me, I will receive 6 superb new titles every month for just £2.75 each, postage and packing free. I am under no obligation to purchase any books and may cancel my subscription at any time. The free books and gift will be mine to keep in any case.

M5ZED

Ms/Mrs/Miss/Mr ....Initials ....

BLOCK CAPITALS PLEASE

Surname ....

Address ....

....

....Postcode...

Send this whole page to:
UK: FREEPOST CN81, Croydon, CR9 3WZ